James Hadley Chase and The Murder Room

>>> This title is part of The Murder Room, our series dedicated to making available out-of-print or hard-to-find titles by classic crime writers.

Crime fiction has always held up a mirror to society. The Victorians were fascinated by sensational murder and the emerging science of detection; now we are obsessed with the forensic detail of violent death. And no other genre has so captivated and enthralled readers.

Vast troves of classic crime writing have for a long time been unavailable to all but the most dedicated frequenters of second-hand bookshops. The advent of digital publishing means that we are now able to bring you the backlists of a huge range of titles by classic and contemporary crime writers, some of which have been out of print for decades.

From the genteel amateur private eyes of the Golden Age and the femmes fatales of pulp fiction, to the morally ambiguous hard-boiled detectives of mid twentieth-century America and their descendants who walk our twenty-first century streets, The Murder Room has it all. >>>

The Murder Room
Where Criminal Minds Meet

themurderroom.com

James Hadley Chase (1906–1985)

Born René Brabazon Raymond in London, the son of a British colonel in the Indian Army, James Hadley Chase was educated at King's School in Rochester, Kent, and left home at the age of 18. He initially worked in book sales until, inspired by the rise of gangster culture during the Depression and by reading James M. Cain's *The Postman Always Rings Twice*, he wrote his first novel, *No Orchids for Miss Blandish*. Despite the American setting of many of his novels, Chase (like Peter Cheyney, another hugely successful British noir writer) never lived there, writing with the aid of maps and a slang dictionary. He had phenomenal success with the novel, which continued unabated throughout his entire career, spanning 45 years and nearly 90 novels. His work was published in dozens of languages and over thirty titles were adapted for film. He served in the RAF during World War II, where he also edited the RAF Journal. In 1956 he moved to France with his wife and son; they later moved to Switzerland, where Chase lived until his death in 1985.

By *James Hadley Chase*
(published in The Murder Room)

No Orchids for Miss Blandish (1939)
Eve (1945)
More Deadly Than the Male (1946)
Mission to Venice (1954)
Mission to Siena (1955)
Not Safe to Be Free (1958)
Shock Treatment (1959)
Come Easy – Go Easy (1960)
What's Better Than Money? (1960)
Just Another Sucker (1961)
I Would Rather Stay Poor (1962)
A Coffin from Hong Kong (1962)
Tell it to the Birds (1963)
One Bright Summer Morning (1963)
The Soft Centre (1964)
You Have Yourself a Deal (1966)
Have This One on Me (1967)
Well Now, My Pretty (1967)
Believed Violent (1968)
An Ear to the Ground (1968)
The Whiff of Money (1969)
The Vulture Is a Patient Bird (1969)
Like a Hole in the Head (1970)

An Ace Up My Sleeve (1971)
Want to Stay Alive? (1971)
Just a Matter of Time (1972)
You're Dead Without Money (1972)
Have a Change of Scene (1973)
Knock, Knock! Who's There? (1973)
Goldfish Have No Hiding Place (1974)
So What Happens to Me? (1974)
The Joker in the Pack (1975)
Believe This, You'll Believe Anything (1975)
Do Me a Favour – Drop Dead (1976)
I Hold the Four Aces (1977)
My Laugh Comes Last (1977)
Consider Yourself Dead (1978)
You Must Be Kidding (1979)
A Can of Worms (1979)
Try This One for Size (1980)
You Can Say That Again (1980)
Hand Me a Fig-Leaf (1981)
Have a Nice Night (1982)
We'll Share a Double Funeral (1982)
Not My Thing (1983)
Hit Them Where It Hurts (1984)

We'll Share a Double Funeral

James Hadley Chase

An Orion book

Copyright © Hervey Raymond 1982

The right of James Hadley Chase to be identified as the author of this work has been asserted in accordance with the Copyright, Designs and Patents Act 1988.

This edition published by
The Orion Publishing Group Ltd
Orion House
5 Upper St Martin's Lane
London WC2H 9EA

An Hachette UK company
A CIP catalogue record for this book is available from the British Library

ISBN 978 1 4719 0412 7

www.orionbooks.co.uk

1

With a sigh of content, Sheriff Ross settled his bulky body into the big armchair before the TV set.

'That was a fine dinner, Mary,' he said, 'and you're a fine cook.'

'Well, as long as you are satisfied,' his wife said as she began to stack the dishes. 'My ma was a better cook, but I reckon I'm not so bad.' She paused to listen to the rain hammering down on the roof of the bungalow. 'What a night!'

Ross, around fifty-three, big, balding, with a pleasant sun-tanned face, nodded agreement.

'About the worst we have had for months.' He reached for his pipe, looking affectionately at his wife, whom he had married some thirty years ago. Regarding her, he remembered her as a young girl, bright-eyed with long dark hair. Now, thirty years on, Mary had filled out, but she still had magic for him. He had often told himself how lucky he had been to have had her as a partner and companion over thirty years.

Ross had had a good, unsensational career. He had left school to become a military policeman, then the war over, he became a Highway Patrol officer, attached to the Miami headquarters, then, because he was liked and trusted, he had been elected Sheriff of Rockville. He wasn't an ambitious man. To be Sheriff of Rockville was no great shakes, but it suited him and, more important, it suited Mary. The money was acceptable, and they were content to live modestly. They had this comfortable bungalow, attached to the Sheriff's office. All Ross had to do was to walk through a doorway from his living-room to reach his office, and he was in business.

Rockville was situated in the north of Florida, amid the citrus-farmers. The town's population was around eight hundred, mostly retired farmers, but there was a sprinkling of young kids only waiting to shake Rockville off their backs and get into some action further south. There was a good self-service store, a bank, a garage, a small church, a school-house and a number of wooden bungalows. The crime rate in Rockville was practically zero. Now and then some kid thieved from the self-service store. Some drunks had to be cooled. The main highway passing through Rockville brought hippies and undesirables on their way south, and often they had to be dealt with. All this was easy for Ross, and he often wondered why he had been given a deputy, who did little except drive around, chat up the out-lying farmers, check on the blacks who worked on the farms and give tickets to the kids who were speeding. All the same, Ross was fond of his deputy: Tom Mason, a young, keen, good-looking twenty-eight-year-old. He and Mason had one evening together each week devoted to the game of chess. Neither of them played well, and it was a turn-and-turn-about who won.

Ross stretched out his long legs and sucked at his pipe which was drawing well and listened to the rain. Some night!

Then feeling guilty that, after a good dinner, he should be already making himself comfortable, he called a little half-heartedly, 'Hi, Mary, are you sure I can't help with the dishes?'

'You stay away!' Mary called back firmly. 'I don't want you in here!'

Ross sucked at his pipe, grinned and relaxed. He thought of tomorrow. He would drive over to Jud Loss's farm, which was situated some fifteen miles from Rockville. Loss's daughter, Lilly, a sixteen-year-old, had been kicking over the traces, according to Miss Hammer, the schoolteacher. Miss Hammer, a dried-up, elderly spinster, had come to Ross and had told him that Lilly, bright

2

enough at school, was keeping undesirable company. The girl was going around with Terry Lepp, the town's Casanova, who owned a powerful Honda motorcycle, and all the girls in town fought each other to have a ride. Miss Hammer had hinted that Terry gave them a lot more than a ride.

Ross had hidden a grin. That was youth. No one was going to stop that kind of thing. Nature is nature. All the same, he was a good friend of Jud Loss who ran a small but prosperous farm. He would go out there and have a careful word in Jud's ear. Maybe the girl could be cooled.

Listening to the sound of the hammering rain, Ross hoped it would cease before morning. A drive out to Loss's farm in weather like this wasn't his idea of fun.

As he tapped ash out of his pipe, he heard the telephone bell ringing.

'Jeff! The telephone!' Mary shouted from the kitchen.

'Yeah. I hear it.' With a sigh, Ross heaved himself out of his chair and, in his stocking feet, padded over to the table on which the telephone stood.

A well-known voice barked in his ear.

'Jeff, we have trouble!'

'Hi, Carl, hell of a night, isn't it? What's the trouble?' Ross asked, knowing he was talking to Carl Jenner, Head of the Highway Patrol.

'This is an emergency, Jeff,' Carl said. 'Haven't time to go into details. I'm calling all local sheriffs. We have a dangerous run-away on our hands. This man, Chet Logan, was being conveyed to Abbeville lock-up. There was an accident. Both police officers with him were killed. Logan has disappeared. This man is dangerous. He just might be heading your way. In this goddamn storm, he'll be difficult to track. I want you to alert every farm in your district to be on guard.'

Ross sucked in his breath.

'Okay, Carl. I'll get busy.'

'Do that. Here's his description: Chet Logan: around five foot ten, powerfully built, blond hair cut in a fringe, age around twenty-three, and he has a cobra snake

3

tattooed on his left forearm. This description will be going out on radio and TV within an hour. He's wearing blue jeans and a brown shirt, but could have found other clothes. This guy is really vicious. He was caught busting a gas station. The patrol officer, trying to arrest him, was stabbed to death, Logan then knifed the gas attendant, who isn't expected to live. He tried to make a getaway, using the patrol officer's motorcycle. He was nabbed as he was trying to get the bike to start. Two patrol officers, alerted by radio by the murdered officer before he investigated what was going on at the gas station, had a rough time with this man. He cut one of them, before the other clubbed him. Now he's loose again. What worries me is he might get to some out-lying farm and get a shotgun. You with me?'

Breathing heavily, Ross tried to assemble his wits. He now wished he hadn't had a second helping of Mary's chicken pie. It was the first time in years he could remember having an emergency like this.

'I'm with you, Carl,' he said, forcing his voice to sound brisk.

'The accident took place at Losseville junction, some twenty miles from you. Logan has been two hours on the run. Warn all out-lying farmers, Jeff, and keep in touch.' Carl Jenner hung up.

Ross slowly replaced the telephone receiver as Mary came into the living-room.

'Something?' she asked, her good-natured face anxious.

'I guess. We've a killer loose,' Ross said. 'Look, Mary, I've got to get busy. Let's have some coffee.' He crossed the room, tugged on his boots, then, opening the door to his office, he turned on the light and sat at his desk.

Mary wasn't one to ask questions. Ross had told her enough. A killer loose! She went immediately to the front door and locked it, then went to the back door and shot the bolt, then she put the kettle on to boil.

Ross made a list of the names and telephone numbers of all the out-lying farmers. He was dialling the telephone number of his deputy, Tom Mason, as Mary brought in a jug of coffee and a cup and saucer.

Although the time was only 21.30, Tom Mason was on his bed with Carrie Smitz, who ran the local post office, under him.

When the telephone bell rang, Tom was thrusting good and deep, and Carrie was squealing with pleasure. The sound of the telephone bell made Tom abruptly cease his activities. He cursed, then broke free from Carrie's frantic and sweaty arms and, swinging off the bed, grabbed the telephone receiver.

The sound of a telephone bell to Tom was like the whistle to a well-trained gun-dog. No matter what was happening, the telephone bell had only to sound and Tom was there.

He heard Ross say, 'Tom! Get over here pronto! We have big trouble,' and Ross hung up.

Carrie sat up on the bed and glared at Tom as, without even looking at her, he began to throw on his clothes.

'What do you imagine you're doing?' she screamed.

'An emergency!' Tom said, zipping up his khaki pants. 'I've got to go.'

'Listen, Stupid,' Carrie yelled. 'Do you remember what we were doing just now?'

Tom zipped up his blouse, then grabbed his gun-belt.

'Sure . . . sure. The old man wants me. I've got to go!'

'Emergency! Some snot-nosed kid's got his dingle in a mangle! Emergency! What emergency is more important . . .'

'Sorry,' Tom said. 'I've got to go.' He dragged on his boots.

'So what do I do?' Carrie demanded. 'Who's going to drive me home in this bloody rain?'

'Just stay put,' Tom said as he scrambled into his slicker. 'Watch your mouth, baby. See you,' and, cramming on his Stetson hat, he plunged out into the rain.

A three-minute drive brought him to the Sheriff's office. As he pulled up, he saw the lights were on. His head bent against the pelting rain, he shoved open the door and entered, rain dripping off his slicker and making small puddles.

Sheriff Ross was talking on the telephone. He hung up as Tom pulled off his slicker.

'What a night!' Tom exclaimed. 'What's the excitement, Jeff?' He moved into the big, old-fashioned office, typical of a small-town Sheriff's office with two cells, a locked gun-rack, two desks and wall hooks on which hung handcuffs.

'Jenner reports there's a killer on the run,' Ross said. 'This guy escaped at Losseville from arrest and could be heading our way. Instructions are to call all out-lying farms in our district and warn the farmers to hide their guns, lock their homes and keep indoors. This guy seems to be real vicious: he killed an officer trying to arrest him and he's killed a gas-station attendant. I've listed the farms to call and the killer's description. You get on the other phone and let's get moving.' He handed Tom a sheet of paper, then began dialling.

This was the first piece of action Tom had experienced since he had been appointed Deputy Sheriff and his eyes lit up. Carrie Smitz forgotten, he went to his desk and pulled the second telephone towards him.

The warning to the farmers took longer than either of the men anticipated. First, the farmers wanted more details. They seemed to take the news as a joke. It wasn't until both Ross and Tom began to bark at them that they slowly came to realise the seriousness of the situation.

'Keep indoors?' one farmer said and laughed. 'Who the hell would want to go out on a night like this? It's raining up here fit to drown a duck.'

'Ted, be serious!' Ross barked. 'Hide your shotgun. This guy could make a break-in. His description will be on TV and radio in a while. This guy's a killer.'

'Well, what the hell do we have cops for?' the farmer demanded. 'If it's that bad, we need protection out here.'

Ross contained his feeling of exasperation.

'Right now, Ted, you've got to look after yourself and your family. There's a big search going on, but he could visit you.'

'If he does, I'll shoot his balls off,' the farmer said, a quaver in his voice.

'Do just that,' Ross said and hung up.

Tom was having the same kind of trouble. The various farmers he called kept asking to speak to Ross, but Tom hammered home the message.

'The Sheriff is calling other folk,' he explained. 'Keep indoors and hide your gun.'

After an hour of this, Ross dialled Jud Loss's number. Loss's farm was the nearest to Rockville and Ross had left him till the last. He had decided first out-lying farms, then the near farms.

Tom had finished his rota. Every farmer on his list had been warned, but he felt frustrated. Why couldn't these dopes understand a simple thing like this? Why must they yak, laugh and not take him seriously?

Ross said, 'I'm not getting any answer from Jud Loss.'

Tom stiffened.

'He's probably in bed.'

'Could be.' Ross listened to the burr-burr sound on the telephone line, settled his big frame more comfortably and waited.

Both men were aware of the sound of the rain hammering on the roof of the office.

'Still no answer,' Ross said.

The two men looked at each other.

'He can't be out,' Tom said uneasily.

'I guess someone should be answering by now. There's Doris and Lilly. They can't all be out.' Ross broke the connection, then dialled again.

Tom became aware that tension was building up in the office. He sat back, watching Ross as he held the receiver to his ear. Finally, after a long three minutes, Ross hung up.

'No one's answering.'

'Do you think . . .?' Tom began and stopped.

'Someone should be answering. I don't like it, Tom.' Ross dialled the number again, but again there was no answer.

'I'll go up there and take a look-see,' Tom said. 'There's nothing for me to do here now.' He reached for his slicker.

'Well, I guess,' Ross said reluctantly. 'Yeah. They could be in trouble. Be careful, Tom. That'll be a nasty drive.'

As Tom put on his slicker, he wasn't thinking about the drive, he was thinking that maybe somewhere around the farm, a run-away, vicious killer might be lurking.

He checked his .38 police special as Ross watched him.

'I'll alert Jenner,' Ross said. 'Maybe he can get a couple of his men up there. I don't like you going up on your own, Tom.'

Tom forced a grin.

'Could be they have their TV at full blast and don't hear the phone,' he said without much hope. 'Still, I'd better check.' He put on his Stetson. 'I'll keep in touch on the radio.'

'I'll be listening. Be careful, Tom.'

'You bet,' and Tom went out into the drowning rain.

Jud Loss's farm consisted of a comfortable bungalow, several barns and a chicken-run. The farm was modest, but thriving. Loss owned some sixty acres of orange-trees and employed three blacks, and, when picking time came, some twenty blacks.

The three permanent blacks had cabins well away from Loss's bungalow. They had been with him for the past ten years. They and their families handled most of the heavy work.

Tom thought of these black people as he drove up the narrow road towards the farm, wrestling with the steering-wheel as his back wheels slipped on the mud, his windshield wipers scarcely able to cope with the pouring rain. What were these blacks doing? Probably at home, glued to the TV. He knew them well. If there was an emergency at the bungalow, he was sure he could rely on them for help.

His big Ford slid in the mud and he again wrestled with the steering-wheel. Not much further. He switched on his radio.

'Sheriff? Mason calling.' Tom was always formal when using the radio.

'Hi, Tom! I'm hearing you.'

'I'm now approaching the farm,' Tom said. 'It's been heavy going. Lots of mud. '

'I'm still trying to contact Loss. Still no answer. Careful how you approach.'

'Yeah. I'm turning off my headlights. I'm on the crest of the hill down to the farm. I can see the farm now. There are lights showing. I guess I'll leave the car and approach on foot.'

'Do that, Tom. Look for trouble. Jenner says there's a patrol car diverted your way, but won't be with you for at least half an hour. Look, Tom, maybe you'd better wait for them.'

'I guess I'll take a look-see, Sheriff. I'll take care. Over and out.'

Tom turned off the radio and switched off his head-lights. He sat staring at the farm bungalow some three hundred yards away. Lights showed in the living-room. Tom often called at the bungalow and knew its geography. To the left was the main bedroom, and in the attic was Lilly's bedroom. There were no lights showing in those two rooms.

Reluctantly he got out of the car, his head ducking against the pelting rain. His hand fumbled under his slicker and he drew his gun. Slowly, he began the muddy walk towards the bungalow, aware he was breathing heavily and his heart was thumping. As he approached the bungalow, he heard the telephone bell ringing faintly through the closed windows of the living-room.

He felt very much alone. Up to this moment, his life as Deputy Sheriff had been easy and straightforward. He had been proud of his uniform, proud to be carrying a gun on his hip, and pleased to be welcomed when he called on the out-lying farms. In his short career of less than three years as Deputy Sheriff, he had never had trouble. Even the drunks had been amiable. Some of the hippy kids had cursed him, but had accepted his authority. Up to now, working with Sheriff Ross in this small town, Rockville, his life had been a bowl of cherries.

But now, standing in the darkness, the rain hammering down on him as he stared uneasily at the lighted windows of the bungalow, still hearing the faint and sinister sound of the telephone bell, sudden fear gripped him. He had never felt such fear before. There had been times, when driving his car, he had avoided a head-on crash, when fear had seized him, but this present fear, that was now gripping him, was something that snatched away his confidence and made his knees shake. He was alarmed how fast his heart was beating, how rapid his breath hissed between his clenched teeth and he could feel cold sweat running down his back, and a tightening cramp in his stomach.

He stood motionless, oblivious to the pelting rain, only aware of his fear. Was the vicious killer in the bungalow? Was he somewhere in the wet darkness, maybe creeping towards him?

The cramp in his stomach worsened. Ross had told him two of Jenner's men were on their way to him. Tom drew in a deep breath. Why take chances? The sensible thing to do was to get back into the car, lock the doors and wait until these men arrived. Hadn't Ross told him to wait?

He began to move to the car, then the faint but persistent sound of the telephone bell was once again to him like the whistle to a well-trained dog.

He turned to face the bungalow. If he hadn't the guts to go down there, he told himself, he would never respect himself. Damn it! He was a Deputy Sheriff! He might even arrest this killer single-handed if the killer was in the bungalow, and at the back of his frightened mind Tom prayed he wouldn't be there.

Holding his gun in a wet, shaky grip, the safety-catch snapped back, he began a slow and cautious advance towards the bungalow.

He paused when he was within fifty feet of the bungalow. He could see the curtains of the lighted living-room were drawn. The sound of the telephone bell was much louder. The sound drew him forward like a beckoning finger.

He passed a clump of bushes, unaware of them in the darkness. He was also unaware of the dark shape of a man, crouching in the bushes, watching him as he moved towards the bungalow.

The cramp in his stomach made Tom pause, then he forced himself again to move forward. With his left hand under his slicker, he unhooked a powerful flashlight from his belt. He sent the beam to the front door and saw it stood ajar. He stopped short. The fact the door stood ajar added to his fear. He looked furtively to right and left into the wet darkness. The only sound, apart from the drumming rain, was the telephone bell that now stretched his nerves. He wished to God it would stop ringing.

Was the killer inside, waiting for him? Why should the front door be ajar unless there was trouble in there?

He peered into the lobby, which was lighted from the light coming from the living-room, its door half open. He could see the steep stairs that led to Lilly's bedroom.

In a small, husky voice, he called, 'Anyone home?' and switched off his flashlight. He waited, then hearing nothing, and after an uneasy glance over his shoulder through the open front door, he shoved the door shut with the heel of his boot and moved into the living-room, familiar to him after so many visits when Jud's wife, Doris, used to invite him for a cup of coffee while he waited for Jud to come from the orchard. He advanced slowly, his gun at the ready, his heart hammering, until he had a clear view of the big room. What he saw made him catch his breath.

By the French window, Doris's big, comfortable body lay face down, her head in a pool of congealing blood. From behind the big settee a pair of boots showed. Scarcely breathing, Tom moved forward and peered around the settee. Jud Loss's short thick body lay face down, a pool of blood matting his thick, ginger-coloured hair.

Tom felt bile rush into his mouth and he gulped, then

11

let the bile spatter on his muddy boots. He was very nearly sick to his stomach, but somehow controlled himself.

He looked wildly around the room, his gun wavering in his hand, but only he, the two bodies and some flies already buzzing excitedly around the pools of blood were the occupants.

Tom had never seen violent death before, and the shock paralysed him. He stood there, staring first at Jud Loss's body and then at Doris's body. With those terrible head wounds, he knew they must be dead.

He stepped back into the lobby.

'Lilly?'

Had she been lucky? Had she been out while this awful thing had happened? He couldn't imagine even Lilly going to Rockville on a night like this.

He looked at the steep flight of stairs, then reaching for the light-switch that lit up the lobby, bracing himself, he climbed the stairs the way an old man with a rickety heart climbs stairs.

The bedroom door at the head of the stairs stood open.

'Lilly?' Tom's voice was a croak.

But for the hammering rain there was silence.

Tom stood at the head of the stairs, unable to move forward. He thought of Lilly Loss. He reckoned she was the prettiest girl in Rockville. Often, he had had ideas about her, and he knew she knew it, but at sixteen she was too young, but that, of course, didn't stop her going around with that creep Ted Lepp. Tom was sure that if he raised a finger Lilly would have jumped into his bed as Carrie Smitz, who was nineteen, was always ready to jump into his bed. Give Lilly a couple of years, and Tom had promised himself he would raise his finger, but now, as he stood before the open doorway, staring into the darkness of Lilly's bedroom, he only felt cold shivers running down his back.

'Lilly?' he said, raising his voice, then he forced himself to move forward and he groped for the light-switch.

Lilly lay face down across the bed, her head a pulpy

mess of blood, brains and hair, her shortie nightdress rucked up, her long slim legs spread wide.

She had been as viciously clubbed to death as her parents had been.

Turning, Tom stumbled down the stairs as the telephone bell began to ring. He was so shocked, his mind was a blank. He moved unsteadily into the living-room, located the telephone and snatched up the receiver. He was vaguely aware that he had dropped his flashlight on the stairs, and as he put the telephone receiver to his ear he laid his gun on the table.

'Is that you, Tom? What's happening?' Ross's voice.

Tom struggled to speak, but he made only stuttering noises. Then he no longer could control the urge to vomit.

'It's Tom,' he managed to say, then, turning his head, he was violently sick on the floor.

He heard Ross shouting, 'Tom! Are you in trouble?'

Tom bent forward, his eyes closed, struggling to speak. Dimly, above the sound of Ross's shouting voice and the hammering of the rain, he heard a sound behind him. He began to look fearfully over his shoulder when he received a crushing blow that descended on his rain-sodden Stetson hat. He fell across the table, unconscious, smashing a leg of the table. He, the wrecked table and the telephone crashed to the floor.

Sergeant Hank Hollis and Patrol Officer Jerry Davis sat side by side in the big patrol car with Hollis driving.

Every man of the Florida Highway Patrol had been pressed into service to find and arrest the escaped killer, Chet Logan.

Davis, aged twenty-five, had been enjoying a chicken dinner, prepared by his pretty wife, when Sergeant Hollis had pulled up outside his bungalow. Five minutes later, Davis, cursing under his breath, had buckled on his gun-belt, thrown on his slicker and Stetson hat and followed Hollis out into the pelting rain.

'Orders to get to Jud Loss's farm fast,' Hollis said, as he

started the car engine. 'You know where it is?'

'I know,' Davis said, his mouth full of half eaten chicken. 'Isn't that swell! Just when I was having dinner!'

'This killer could be there. Tom Mason's investigating,' Hollis said, edging the car onto the highway. 'He's asking for support.'

'These goddamn deputy sheriffs,' Davis growled. 'Can't they do anything without us?'

'If the killer's there, Mason will need support.'

'Yeah? *If* he's there, but suppose he ain't? A nice ten-mile drive in this goddamn rain just to hold Mason's hand.'

'Stop griping, Jerry, this is a job!' Hollis said, a snap in his voice. 'Every man on the force is out in this rain. Logan's got to be caught!'

'Okay, so we catch him. How many medals do we get?' Davis muttered, then shrugged. 'A mile ahead, Sarge, there's a turning on the left, and then up a dirt road. In this rain, the road will be a beauty. Then five miles further on, if we get that far, there's a fork in the road and we go left, and another five miles, if we haven't bogged down, it brings us to Loss's farm.' He leaned back, switched on the radio to report to the dispatcher at headquarters their position.

The drive was dangerous and slow. Once off the highway, Hollis struck mud. Every now and then the car got into a skid which Hollis corrected with expert ease. As the car began to climb, the mud increased, but Hollis kept going, skidding more often.

'Man! Am I loving this!' Davis exclaimed after a while. 'Here's the fork. Keep left. We've only got another five bloody miles to go.'

'I've known worse,' Hollis said, wrestling the car out of another skid. 'I remember . . .'

The radio came to life. Headquarter's dispatcher said, 'Calling car ten. Come in, car ten.'

Both Hollis and Davis became alert.

Davis said, 'Car ten. Hearing you.'

'Report from Sheriff Ross of Rockville. Something's

badly wrong at Loss's farm. Mason's there. Last contact is he was approaching the farm. No reply on his radio. Sounds on the telephone, before it packed up, indicate a struggle. We are diverting two patrol cars to you. Approach with caution. Logan is highly dangerous.'

'Hear you and out,' Davis said. He opened his slicker and loosened his gun in its holster. 'Maybe this sonofabitch *is* there after all.'

Taking chances, Hollis increased the speed of the car. The tyres bit tarmac and the car surged forward for a mile or so, then hit mud again and Hollis had to start wrestling.

'Man! Did I choose the wrong job!' Davis exclaimed. 'Franklin has it dead easy. He sits in the dry and yaks while we poor sods do the work.'

Hollis reduced speed. In less than ten minutes, they began to climb the crest of the hill.

'We're nearly there, Sarge.'

Hollis snapped off his headlights and slowed the car. He edged the car forward and pulled up beside Mason's big Ford.

Davis went on the air.

'Car ten has arrived. We can see the farm. Lights are showing. We're right by Mason's car.' He lowered his window and peered at the big Ford, feeling the rain beating against his face. 'Mason's not in his car. We're investigating. Over and out,' and he snapped off the radio.

The two men spilled out of their car into the pelting rain.

'I'll go first,' Hollis said, drawing his gun. 'Give me two minutes, then follow me. You move around to the back. If Logan is still in there and makes a bolt, I want you at the back. Take no chances with him.'

'I don't imagine he is there,' Davis said, 'but you watch it, Sarge.'

Moving fast, Hollis began to run down the crest. Davis waited until Hollis had nearly reached the bungalow, then he set off fast across the sodden, muddy grass, circling around to the back of the bungalow.

Reachi..g the open front door of the bungalow, Hollis paused to listen, but except for the drumming of the rain no sound came to him.

During his move up to the rank of Sergeant, Hollis had faced many dangerous situations. He was a man without nerves. He was determined, if Logan was in the bungalow, that this would be the end of his vicious road.

Moving silently, his gun at the ready, Hollis entered the lighted lobby, rain from his slicker making puddles on the polished floor that Doris Loss had taken so much pride in keeping immaculate.

Cautiously, he peered into the living-room. The first thing he saw was Tom Mason's body, lying face down amid the wreckage of the table. Hollis didn't move. He stared at Mason, and unpleasant facts registered in his alert mind.

Mason should have been wearing his Stetson hat, his slicker and his gun-belt. He wasn't wearing any of these articles.

Hollis's mind moved swiftly. If Logan was here or had been here, he had taken Mason's hat, slicker and gun!

Was he still in the bungalow? Logan was now armed with a .38 revolver and a cartridge belt!

Hollis slammed back the door and jumped into the room. Looking around swiftly, he saw only the bodies of Jud and Doris Loss. He backed out of the room, moved across the lobby and kicked open the dark bedroom door. That room was empty. Moving cautiously, he checked the kitchen and the bathroom, then returned to the lobby. He regarded the steep stairs, leading to Lilly's bedroom. Was Logan up there? Crouching, his gun pushed forward, Hollis climbed the stairs, paused at the open bedroom door, then edged forward and reached for the light-switch. It took him only seconds to assure himself Logan wasn't in the bungalow. He paused for a moment to stare at Lilly's body, then, turning, he rushed down the stairs and into the rain. He bawled for Davis who came from around the back of the bungalow at a run.

'He's skipped,' Hollis said. 'We have a goddamn massacre inside. Take a look.'

The two men entered the living-room. While Davis checked the bodies of Jud and Doris, Hollis bent over Mason.

'He's still alive,' he said, squatting on his heels.

'These two ain't.' Davis came to kneel by Mason. He turned him gently. 'Hit on the head like the other two.'

'The girl's dead. She's upstairs.' Hollis straightened. 'We've got to get help. Use the telephone.'

Davis snatched up the telephone from the floor, then cursed. The connecting wire hung loose.

'The sonofabitch is playing it smart.'

'Sure is. He's stolen Mason's hat, slicker and gun.' Hollis said. 'In that disguise . . .'

'Listen!'

The two men paused.

Faintly, above the sound of the rain, they heard a car engine start up.

'He's getting away!' Hollis shouted.

Both men, slipping and sliding in the mud, raced up the crest.

The sound of a car, moving fast in low gear, was now fading as the two men reached their car. Mason's car was no longer there.

'Call Jenner!' Hollis said, scrambling into the car. 'We'll go after him! We could catch him, but alert Jenner!'

As Davis got in the car, Hollis switched on the ignition, then pressed down the gas pedal. Nothing happened.

Davis was pressing the radio button, but no light appeared.

'He's fixed the radio!' he snarled, groped and found trailing wires.

Hollis was already out of the car and peering with the aid of his flashlight into the engine.

'He's taken the distributor head!'

The sound of the retreating car had now faded away.

'We've got to get to a telephone,' Davis said. 'Loss must have a car!'

'Yes. You go, Jerry, I'll take care of Mason. Franklin said two cars were coming, but God knows how long they'll take.'

As Davis ran towards the three barns in search of Loss's car, Hollis returned to the bungalow. He knelt by Mason's side. Lifting him, he saw Mason's eyes open.

'Did he get away?' Mason mumbled, then his eyes closed and he sank back into unconsciousness.

Hollis snatched a pillow from the settee and put it under Mason's head, then went out into the lobby and peered into the wet darkness.

He waited several minutes, then he saw Davis running towards him.

'Loss's car and the truck are out of action,' he said, coming into the lobby. 'Looks as if we're stuck, Sarge.'

Hollis grunted.

'Franklin said two cars were coming. So we wait.'

'And the sonofabitch gets away!'

'He won't get far.' Hollis walked into the living-room and pulled off his slicker. 'We'll get him.' He looked down at Mason. 'This poor guy needs fast medical treatment. He's in a bad way.'

Davis looked down at Mason.

'Think he's going to croak?'

'I don't know. I guess he was wearing his hat when he was hit. This punk can hit.' Hollis glanced at the bodies of Jud and Doris and grimaced. 'A real, vicious killer.'

'Suppose our guys don't make it?' Davis said. 'Look, there's a telephone-box at the end of the road. How about that?'

'That's five miles, Jerry. No, we wait. With luck our guys could arrive any minute.'

'Yeah. Okay, so we wait.'

Neither of the men was to know that the two patrol cars heading their way had run into trouble. Both of the drivers, driving too fast, had skidded in the thick mud. The leading car got out of control and crashed into a ditch. The second car just managed to stop to find the driver of the first car had a broken arm. In the pelting rain, the driver of the second car managed to tow the first car out of the ditch, then, leaving it, he continued on towards Loss's farm.

There had been over an hour's delay.

Chet Logan, wearing Mason's slicker and hat with Mason's gun on the seat beside him, drove along the highway, safe for the moment from pursuit.

2

As Perry Weston drove his Hertz rental Toyota along the almost deserted highway, his headlights scarcely coping with the pelting rain, his windshield-wipers working furiously, he listened on the car radio to some woman screaming pop with a drummer and a saxophone player sounding as if they were out of their minds.

Perry was drunk enough not to care about the screeching voice nor the rain. He had been warned at Jacksonville airport that the weather was turning bad, and he must expect to encounter very heavy rain.

He had smiled at the Hertz girl.

'Who cares about rain?' he had said. 'Who cares about anything?'

Well, it was certainly raining, that was for sure. Tomorrow, he told himself hopefully, there would be blue skies and hot sunshine.

He had come from New York and, during the flight down to Jacksonville, he had been drinking Scotch on the rocks steadily, to the concern of the air hostess who kept giving him a refill. At the Jacksonville airport he had bought a bottle of Ballantine to be his companion for the long drive to Rockville. Well, he told himself, it wasn't all that long: some seventy miles, but this rain was forcing him to drive at a crawl.

He looked at the clock on the lighted dashboard. The time was 21.05. Although Perry wasn't to know it, at this exact time both Sheriff Ross and Deputy Tom Mason were telephoning the out-lying farms, warning the farmers there was a vicious killer loose.

Maybe, Perry thought as he stared at the rain hammering down on the highway, he should have stayed over at Jacksonville. Although he had been warned about the coming rain-storm, he hadn't bargained for this goddamn down-pour. Feeling the Scotch dying on him, he pulled up at the side of the highway. He searched and found the bottle of Ballantine, unscrewed the cap and took a long swig from the bottle.

Better, he thought, as he rescrewed the cap. He lit a cigarette. The woman was still screeching over the radio and he became aware of her raucous voice. He switched stations. The voice of a man, desperately trying to imitate the voice of Bing Crosby, filled the car. After listening for a few moments, Perry grimaced and turned off the radio. He took another swig at the bottle, then put the bottle back into the glove compartment. He stubbed out his cigarette and lit another. He felt relaxed and pleasantly drunk. There was no hurry, he told himself. If he reached his fishing-lodge any time this night, so what?

His mind shifted to the events of yesterday. How long into the past those events seemed now!

Well, he thought, those events certainly started this trip down to his fishing-lodge which he had bought some three years ago. It was an isolated wooden structure, right by the river, surrounded by trees and flowering shrubs and some two miles from the village of Rockville. He had bought it for practically nothing, but had spent money on it. It had two bedrooms, a big living-room, and he had put in a modern bathroom and a fully equipped kitchen. He had planned, when he wasn't working in NYC, he would relax at the lodge, fishing for black bass, cooking for himself and enjoying a solitude that was rare in New York. It hadn't worked out like that. It was now two years since he had visited the fishing-lodge. He had made the fatal mistake to have married a girl fifteen years his junior. It wasn't her scene to spend two months in some dreary fishing-lodge, miles from the bright lights, while he fished. He accepted that, but there were often times when he thought of that peaceful river, the silence, the excitement of landing a black bass and cooking it for a late dinner. He had now been married for two years. He had done his best, but Sheila was one of those young girls who were never satisfied. She hated him going into his study to work. She was always interrupting, demanding to be taken to some place or the other: places that bored him out of his mind. A fatal marriage, he told himself. Once the glamour of her young, beautiful body became routine, he realised how far, mentally, they were apart.

Then yesterday!

When Sheila and he were having a shouting match: something that was now happening pretty well every day, the telephone bell had rung. Sheila had picked up a small Chinese vase which Perry valued and had thrown it at him. He had dodged and the vase smashed against the wall.

Perry had said, 'Get out of my sight!'

'You're a goddamn drunk!' Sheila had screamed, and had run out of the room, slamming the door.

The telephone bell was persistent. For a long moment Perry had stared at the shattered pieces of Chinese porcelain, then he had crossed the room and answered the telephone.

'Mr Weston?' A woman's cool voice.

'Yes.'

'This is Mr Hart's secretary, Mr. Weston.'

Startled, Perry said, 'Oh . . . why, hello, Grace. How's life with you?'

'Mr Hart would be glad to see you this morning at eleven o'clock,' Grace Adams said. She always spoke on the telephone as if she had the President of the United States waiting on another line. 'Mr Hart will be leaving in three hours for Los Angeles. Please be punctual.'

When the President of the Rad-Hart Movie Corporation asked to see you, you said yes, even if you were in hospital with a broken leg.

'I'll be there,' Perry said, and tried to beat Grace Adams to the cut-off, but he was a split second too late. She was an expert at terminating a telephone conversation.

Sitting in the Toyota, with the rain pouring down, Perry grimaced. The interview with Silas S. Hart had been sticky. Thinking about the meeting, Perry reached into the glove compartment and took another swig at the bottle.

Silas S. Hart and he had always got along well; there was a reason. For the past four years, Perry had provided Hart with original film scripts that had made big money for the Rad-Hart Movie Corporation.

Hart had the reputation for ruthlessness and toughness, but, up to now, he appeared to treat Perry as his son. This surprised Perry as he had heard so many tales about the way Hart had treated other script-writers who had failed to make the grade, but to him Hart was like an affectionate father. In his bones, Perry knew this attitude of Hart's was because he had given Hart four money-making scripts. Fair enough, but what would happen if the next script that was already in Hart's hands turned out a flop?

A couple of months ago, Hart and Perry had talked about a future film.

'This time I want something with blood and guts,' Hart had said. 'We now have to give these morons who pay at the box office something to make them wet their pants. How do you feel about it? Do you think you can give me something like that? I want something with lots of action, blood and sex. Go away and think about it. Let me have an outline in a couple of months. Okay?'

'You don't mean a horror film?' Perry asked.

'That's the last thing I want. I want ordinary people in a situation that is packed with action, blood and sex. Ordinary people, you understand. A situation that can happen to anyone, like being held hostage, like a bunch of thugs moving into their home, like a drunk driver killing a child and trying to cover up. That kind of situation, but none of those. They've been done and done. Think about it. With your talent, you'll come up with a humdinger. Okay?'

'Sure,' Perry said. You don't show a lack of confidence

when talking to Silas S. Hart, not if you wanted to stay his favourite script-writer. 'I'll think about it, and let you have an outline of my thinking. Right?'

Hart smiled.

'That's the boy! And, Perry, it's worth fifty thousand, plus five per cent of the producer's profit. This will be a big deal for you, and a big deal for me.'

For two months, Perry had struggled to invent an original plot that would satisfy his boss. During those two months, Sheila had been at her worst. Perry had explained to her that he had to invent a plot that would bring in big money,. so please relax and give him a chance to think, but Sheila wouldn't leave him alone. At this time, there was a two-week film gala on, and she wanted to show herself off with Perry every night.

'I'm the wife of the best script-writer in this goddamn city,' she had screamed. 'What will those snobs think if they don't see us?'

The gala sessions went on until three o'clock in the morning, and Perry had come home so drunk that Sheila had to drive. The following mornings he was nursing a hangover, then in the afternoons, while Sheila was playing tennis, he tried to put on paper a slim idea that might – just might – please Silas S. Hart.

Finally, drunk, he had typed out the outline and had sent it to Grace Adams. He was now quarrelling with Sheila so continuously that he ceased to care.

As he sat in the Toyota, with rain hammering down on the car's roof, he thought about his wife. What a stupid sucker he had been to have married her! He had been completely carried away by her vivacity, her sensuality and her youth. The fact that all his unmarried men friends were scrambling for her acted as a crazy challenge to his ego. She hadn't been easy to win. She had played hard to get. The red light should have warned him what he was in for, but he was besotted, and he had won her against heavy odds. He was making big money and was able to go along with her constant demands. At first she was marvellous in bed. His first three months, married to her, had been exciting and he had basked in his friends' envy. Then her demands began to worry him. He had his work. Sheila did nothing except swim, play tennis and yak. God! he thought, what a non-stop yakker! When he was wrestling with a script, she would come into his study, sit on his desk and yak about her girl friends, who was sleeping with whom, what nightclub they'd go to that night, how about a trip to Fort Lauderdale to get some sun? He had pointed out, with growing impatience, that he was working. Sheila had stared at him, then gave him a thin little smile and left him. That was when she moved into the second bedroom.

'You need your work,' she had said, staring at him, her China-blue eyes cold. 'I need my sleep.'

Perry had found consolation in a bottle of Ballantine. When Silas S. Hart had asked to see him, Perry felt like a man driving to his doom. The sketchy outline of his script he had sent Hart, he knew was something any third-rate script-writer would have thrown together.

As he rode up in the elevator to the Rad-Hart Movie Corporation's offices, he cursed himself for sending Hart such utter crap. It was only because of his rows with Sheila and the Ballantine that had made him do it. It would have been much wiser to have admitted to Hart that he just wasn't in the mood to produce and not to have sent him anything.

He lit another cigarette as he stared through the windshield at the drowning rain.

Hart had given him his usual warm welcome, waving him to a chair, sitting back in his big executive chair, his fleshy, tough-looking face smiling.

'I haven't much time, Boy,' Hart said. 'I have to get to LA. There are finks there causing trouble, but I wanted to have a word with you.'

Hart always called Perry 'Boy', and Perry believed it was a term of affection.

'Want a drink?' Hart asked. 'Don't say no, because I do.'

He pressed a button, and Grace Adams appeared. She

was tall, thin, around forty, always immaculately dressed, and her pale face looked as if it had been carved from a slab of ivory. She produced two Scotches on the rocks and went away.

'Well, Boy,' Hart went on, 'we won't talk about this thing you sent me, we will talk about you. Okay?'

'If you say so,' Perry said woodenly. Although he longed for a drink, he let the glass stand on the desk.

'Suppose we start this little session,' Hart said, after sipping his drink, 'by me saying you are the best original script-writer I have been lucky to have. Together, we have made a lot of money. I consider you a valuable property in my Corporation. When I have asked you to deliver, up to now, you have always delivered.' He paused to sip his drink, then went on, 'Apart from being a valuable property, I like you. I seldom like the people who work for me, knowing they don't like me, but I like you.' He smiled, then finished his drink. 'Well, Boy, I have been keeping an eye on you. When I have a property as valuable as you, I'm like some woman with a two-million-dollar diamond. She keeps an eye on it, so I arranged to keep an eye on you.'

Perry picked up his glass and drained it.

'That's your privilege,' he said, setting down the glass.

'Yes. It seems you have two problems that are interfering with your work. The big one is your wife. The smaller one is drink. Right?'

'I don't want to discuss my wife with anyone,' Perry said, curtly.

'That's a normal reaction.' Hart moved his bulk to a more comfortable position in his chair. 'Not *anyone*; that doesn't include me. I'm special, and I look on you as a partner. Now, when a man of thirty-eight marries a girl of twenty-three, and this man is a real inspired worker, he is in natural trouble. Girls of twenty-three want the bright lights of life especially when they have married men with your kind of money. Bright lights and creative work don't marry, nor does hitting the bottle.'

'I'm not in the mood to listen to this,' Perry said. 'Did

you or didn't you like the outline I sent you?'

Hart reached for a cigar, stared at it, cut it and lit it.

'Did you?'

'Okay,' Perry said. 'So what? I tried, but it didn't work. Get someone else to do it.'

'That's not the solution, Boy. That's backing out, and you're not a quitter. Right?'

'I'd rather you got someone else. I have enough to handle without some goddamn movie script.'

'That's how the situation looks to you, but not to me. There's always a solution to any problem if you look and think hard enough. I want you to co-operate. I know you can dream up the script I want. I know that, but you can't do it if you are bothered by your wife.'

Perry got to his feet and walked the length of the big room, then he returned to Hart's desk.

'I would rather you got someone else and leave me to handle Sheila.'

'You're not going to handle her, Boy,' Hart said. 'She's going to be a pest. I have had a report on her. She has her hooks into you, and she's not going to let go until you have no more money to spend on her, then she'll walk out and find another sucker. I know her a lot better than you do. I've had reports on her background and reports of what she is doing while you try to write something worthwhile. She has two boyfriends. I have their names, but that doesn't matter. She screws around, Boy. You think she plays tennis every afternoon? She doesn't. She is shacked up with one of these men, having it off. All she's bothered about is your money. These other two finks haven't money. If they had, she would have left you before now. My people bugged the motel room where she has it off. I have a tape, but you won't want to listen to it. You've picked a real bad one, Boy. I'm sorry to tell you this, but I need you and you need me. Right?'

Perry sat down abruptly.

'I don't believe a word of this,' he muttered.

'You do believe it, Boy,' Hart said quietly, 'but, naturally, you don't want to believe it. I wouldn't either, but I don't make mistakes. You have to get rid of Sheila. You have to make up your mind that this is your only solution. My people can give you all the evidence for a divorce. Once you are rid of her, you'll get back to your normal writing self.'

Perry stiffened.

'I am not going to discuss Sheila with you nor anyone else,' he said, a snap in his voice. 'This is my personal problem, and I'm not having anyone trying to solve it for me.'

Hart nodded.

'Before I asked you to come to see me, I did some thinking. I felt sure you would say just what you've said. It's your personal problem, and you don't want interference. Okay. I would have been disappointed if you had said otherwise. Now, will you do me a favour?'

Perry looked suspiciously at this big man, resting in his executive chair.

'A favour?'

'Yes. To both of us.'

'What's the favour then?'

'You like fishing?'

'Sure, but what has fishing to do with this?'

'You have a fishing-lodge in Florida some place?'

Perry stared.

'How did you know that?'

'Never mind. You have, haven't you?'

'Yes.'

'Right. I want you to go down there today. I want you to fish and think. I want you to tell your wife that you have been sent by me on location to work on the script you have given me. As a favour to me and to yourself, do this. Get her out of your mind. Get off the bottle. Fish and think. I told you I want something with action, blood and sex. You sit by the river with a rod in your hand and you'll produce what I want. Will you do this?'

Listening, Perry realised that this was what he wanted to do: to get away from NYC, away from Sheila and re-find himself in the solitude of the fishing-lodge with no one to bother him: just himself, a rod and an idea for a script to think about.

He smiled.

'Okay. You have a deal,' he said.

He returned home in time to catch Sheila who was about to leave for a game of tennis. He told her he was flying that afternoon to Los Angeles with Silas S. Hart. He would be going on location, and maybe, he would be away a couple of months. He expected a scene, but Sheila merely shrugged. Looking at her, he saw excitement growing in her China-blue eyes, and he felt a sudden cold dislike for her.

'So what do I do?' she asked. 'Sit around while you're having it off with some tart?'

'You must please yourself what you do. This is a job, Sheila. I have to go.'

'I can imagine. What do I do about money?'

'I'll leave you enough.' He wrote out a cheque for seven thousand dollars and gave it to her.

'You call this enough for two months?' she had said.

'Everything is paid for by the bank, Sheila. That's more than enough,' and leaving her, he went up the stairs to his bedroom. As he began to pack, he heard her car drive away.

Once you are rid of her, you'll get back to your normal writing self.

And now, sitting in the Toyota, listening to the rain hammering down on the roof of the car, he nodded to himself. Well, he was rid of her for two months. It remained to be seen if he got back to his normal writing self.

On the telephone, Sheriff Ross was talking to Carl Jenner.

'Look, Carl, what the hell's happening?' he demanded. 'I can't raise Tom nor your men. What's happening?'

'I don't know. Hollis and Davis don't reply. The telephone at the farm is dead.'

'For God's sake! I know that! I've been trying that

telephone for the past hour! What are you doing?'

'I've diverted two cars to the farm, Jeff. One of them slid off the road and into a ditch. The driver has a broken arm. The other car stopped to pull the ditched car free, but now the second car is on its way. This is a hell of a night. Lewis and Johnson, in the second car, don't know the way to the farm. They keep reporting they are on farm tracks and the going is fierce.'

'I'm going to the farm to see for myself!' Ross snapped. 'I've had enough of this balls-up! I know the road to the farm backwards. I'll keep in contact with you on radio.'

'Don't do that, Jeff!' Jenner said. 'Wait. Lewis and Johnson can't be that long. I've redirected them. With luck, they should reach the farm in twenty minutes or so.'

'That's not good enough. I'm worried sick about Tom. I'm going!' Ross hung up.

Mary, who had been listening, came into the office with Ross's slicker and hat.

'You'll be careful, Jeff,' she said. 'I'll stand by the telephone.'

He smiled at her.

'Spoken like a true wife of a sheriff,' he said, put on his slicker, checked his gun, then slapped on his hat. 'Don't worry. I know that road inside out.' He gave her a kiss. 'Keep the radio on. I'll be in touch,' and he plunged out into the rain.

The road up to Loss's farm had deteriorated since Tom Mason had tackled the drive, and Ross had to struggle to keep the patrol car from sliding into the ditches either side of the road. Driving slowly, he finally reached the crest of the hill where he found Hollis's car. He switched on full headlights, lighting up the front of the bungalow. A moment later, he saw two men come to the front door and wave to him.

He pulled up outside the bungalow and got out.

'Hi, Sheriff,' Hollis said. 'Glad you made it. So far, my lot haven't shown up.'

Ross grunted and moved into the lobby, out of the rain.

'What's going on? Why haven't you been in contact with Jenner? Where's Tom Mason?'

'Is your car radio operating, Sheriff?'

'Yes, but . . .'

'I've got to report to Jenner,' Hollis said. 'Davis will show you the mess in here,' and he dashed out into the rain and scrambled into Ross's car. In minutes, he was talking to Jenner, telling him of the situation at the farm.

Jenner listened in stunned silence. .

'This escapee has gone off in Mason's car, wearing Mason's hat, slicker, and he's taken Mason's gun,' Hollis concluded.

'This punk must be out of his skull!' Jenner exploded. 'This makes five murders he's committed in one night! Okay, I'll handle it. I'll get an ambulance and the MO. up to you fastest,' and he hung up.

Returning to the bungalow, Hollis found Ross on one knee beside Tom Mason.

'Better not touch him,' Hollis said. 'An ambulance is on its way. He looks real bad.'

'He's dead,' Ross said in a cold, flat voice. 'He just had time to recognise me, then he went.'

Sheila Weston sipped her dry martini while she regarded the handsome man sitting opposite her at a table overlooking the tennis courts.

'You play a fine game of tennis, Mrs Weston,' the man said and smiled. 'Way out of my class. I hope, if it won't bore you, we could play again soon.'

Sheila was in almost a professional class at tennis, and this man who had suggested they might play had offered no opposition. That didn't matter. She liked to win, and especially against a man.

This man, tall with curly dark hair, a handsome suntanned face, had introduced himself as Julian Lucan. Sheila had regarded him and decided he could be an exciting bed partner. After Perry had gone upstairs to pack and she was driving to the tennis club, she had decided she now wanted a change of bed partners. Joey and George were beginning to bore her.

This handsome man could enliven her sex life while Perry was away, she told herself. Seeing the way he was looking at her, she knew there would be no problem.

However, he was a stranger to her. She hadn't seen him at the club before, and she decided to probe a little.

'You don't come here often?'

'First time,' Lucan said. 'Nice here, isn't it? I drove out on the off chance of getting a game. Most days, I'm bottled up in the City.'

She probed further.

'What do you do in the City?'

'I'm a photographer's model. The season's approaching for men's wear, and I'm kept pretty busy.'

She nodded. That seemed satisfactory.

'Are you doing anything over the week-end?'

He gave her a wide, handsome smile.

'Not if you have something more interesting to suggest, Mrs Weston.'

She believed in the direct approach. She had done this before and it always paid off. The well-built men on the beach. The good-looking men at the club bar. She let them take her somewhere: generally to a motel, but this time, she decided, she would make the arrangement.

'Well, I'm all alone this weekend. My husband is away on business.' She smiled. 'Or so he tells me. Would you like to spend tonight and tomorrow at my place?'

His smile widened.

'Nothing I would like better.'

She opened her bag, took out her card-case, slid out a card and pushed it across the table.

'That's the address. Come at eight o'clock. My help will have gone by then. We'll have a cold supper.'

He picked up the card, studied it, then slipped it into his shirt pocket.

'I'll be there, Mrs Weston. I look forward to it.'

'You may call me Sheila, Julian,' she said. 'I have a lunch date. See you tonight,' and giving him a flashing smile, she got to her feet, waved to him and walked to the club house.

Lucan finished his drink, then ordered another. Mrs Perry Weston, the wife of the successful script-writer! Lucan made it his business to know about successful men. Weston must be worth a sack of loot, he thought. Well, his friends called him 'Lucky Lucan'. He seemed to be living up to his name.

Neither Sheila nor Lucan had noticed a thickset man, sitting under a sun-umbrella, nursing a glass of beer. He was one of those nondescript men you pass in the street and not notice. His name was Ted Fleichman, one of The Acme Investigation's best private detectives.

For the past week, he had been instructed to keep tabs on Sheila Weston. A daily, detailed report of her activities was to be sent to a Miss Grace Adams of the Rad-Hart Movie Corporation.

Fleichman had watched Sheila give Lucan her card, then he had watched her make her way to the open air restaurant. He nodded to himself, then, getting to his feet, he went in search of a telephone. He called The Acme Investigations's office and spoke briefly to Dorrie Roper who was in charge of assignments.

'Dorrie, I want Fred Small. Is he around?'

'When isn't he? He's lolling around in the lounge, gaping at the girlie mags. What do you want him for?'

'I need a second on the Weston job. Tell him to hustle down to the Long Island Tennis Club pronto. I'll meet him on the terrace.'

He hung up and returned to his seat under the sun-umbrella.

Julian Lucan was eating a sandwich, relaxing in the sun. He seemed set for a while. From where he sat, Fleichman could see Sheila talking with three other women as they sat at a lunch-table. He nodded. She was settled too for a while. He finished his beer and waved to a waiter for a refill.

Half an hour later, Fred Small, a man in his late fifties, wearing a pale-blue light-weight suit, yet another of the Acme men who could pass in a crowd without being noticed, joined Fleichman.

'What's cooking, Ted?' he asked as he sat beside Fleichman.

'The party across the way in the tennis outfit,' Fleichman said, without looking in Lucan's direction.

Small took a quick, casual glance, then he smiled.

'Oh, him. Lucky Lucan. Man! There's a smooth operator! I had a little trouble with him in Manhattan. Usually, he works the big City.'

'What's his thing, Fred?'

'With those looks, he takes the older women for a ride. All very smooth. He screws them, and then puts on the pressure, gets them either to pay up or give him a big present. He does well.'

'Well, he seems to be having a go at Mrs Weston.' Fleichman grimaced. 'Or maybe, she's having a go at him. Keep tabs on him, Fred. I'll watch her.'

'You know something, Ted? You and I would be on the bread-line if women behaved themselves. Nasty thought, isn't it?'

'Don't leave the men out. It's the way of modern behaviour. We'll never be on the bread-line so long as we can watch and wait.'

Seeing Julian Lucan get to his feet and move over to the waiter to settle his check, Small grabbed up Fleichman's beer, drained it and patted Fleichman on his massive shoulder.

'Get yourself another, Ted. You've got it soft,' and he walked casually after Lucan.

Lunch finished, Sheila parted with her three women friends, then went to a call booth. She spoke to Liza, her coloured help-cum-cook.

'I want to give Mrs Bensinger supper at home, Liza.' she said 'Something nice. I leave it to you. Then get off. Have a nice week-end,' and she hung up.

She then went to the changing-rooms, put on a bikini and went to sit by the swimming-pool. Fleichman sat under another sun-umbrella in view of the pool and waited. His job consisted of waiting, but the money was good and he was a patient man.

As Sheila lay in the sun, her eyes closed behind her big sun-goggles, she thought about Julian Lucan. Some man! she thought, and felt the urge of sex surge through her. Way out of Joey's and George's class. This man could be the lover of all lovers! Those grey, sexy eyes, his muscles and his confidence!

'That was a lovely hunk of man you were talking to,' a voice said.

Frowning, she looked up to find Mavis Bensinger had taken a lounging chair beside her. She and Mavis were confidantes. Mavis had married a man twenty years older than she, but although he was fat and balding and had the disgusting habit of sweating in bed, he was rich. Mavis looked elsewhere for romance. Happily Bensinger spent a lot of his time in Washington, so there were only a few days in the month when he pestered Mavis.

'I guess,' Sheila said with a satisfied smile. 'I'll know tonight. I've invited him home. Perry is in LA.'

'Home?' Mavis sounded startled. 'Is that wise, Sheila? I thought you went to a motel as I do.'

'I'm sick of motels.'

'But suppose one of your creepy-crawly neighbours saw him? You don't want a divorce, do you?'

'Sometimes I think I do. Perry and I are always fighting. We haven't slept together for a couple of months. I think I'd like to be free. There are so many men to choose from.'

'But think of the money Perry makes! He does spoil you. You might not find another man all that easy with money.'

'Oh, shut up!' Sheila got up. 'I'm taking a swim.'

'Well, baby, it's your funeral. I wouldn't divorce Sam. I have only to put up with him for three or four days a month, and I can spend what I like.'

Sheila took a header into the pool.

She returned to her home at 19.00 to find Liza laying the table.

'I got a nice hors d'oeuvres and two good lobsters, Mrs Weston,' she said. 'Will that be all right?'

35

'That's fine,' Sheila said. 'You get off when you've finished. I'm taking a bath.'

She spent the next half hour making herself seductive, and she was an expert at that. As she was fixing her false eyelashes, she heard Liza drive away. Now, she had her home to herself!

At exactly 20.00 Julian Lucan arrived in his rented Mercedes 200 SL. Sheila was standing on the open patio and pointed to the double garage.

Lucan drove his car into the garage beside her Volvo, then he got out of his car, closed the garage door and walked quickly to where she was standing.

'Hello, there,' he said, smiling. 'Well, here I am.'

The small but luxurious house was screened by high hedges and trees. There was no problem of the neighbours seeing Lucan's arrival.

That Saturday night with Lucan was the most exciting Sheila had ever experienced. For the first time in her life a man left her completely exhausted. His sexual technique was, to Sheila, like a shot of LSD. She floated away under him, out of her body, which he manipulated in a way that made her cry out, clutch him and groan for more.

She came out of a heavy sleep to find him dressing. For a long moment she didn't know what was happening. Then she remembered it was Sunday and, looking at her bedside clock, she saw the time was 11.50.

'You're not leaving?' she asked in dismay, sitting up in bed. 'It's early yet.'

He smiled at her.

'Yes, honey, I have a date in the City.'

'But it's Sunday!'

'That's right. These people don't keep Sundays.' He stood before the mirror of her dressing-table and adjusted his tie.

Looking at his long, strong back, Sheila released a long, moaning sigh.

'I'll get you coffee.' Naked, she swung off the bed and put on a wrap.

36

'I'd love that, honey,' he said. 'Did you have a good time?'

'You don't have to ask . . . didn't you?'

'I sure did.'

While she was heating up the coffee which Liza had prepared, she thought of the past night. This had been a fantastic experience! She mustn't lose this fantastic lover! It was a shock to hear he wasn't staying until Monday morning, but although she was only twenty-three years of age, she did know that to put pressure on a man was fatal. Next time, they would go to a motel. Then the next weekend, when she could get rid of Liza, they would come here.

She carried a tray of coffee and cups into the living-room to find Lucan wandering around, staring at the various objets d'art that Perry had collected. To her irritation, Perry was a collector, and, even more irritating, he knew good antiques.

'It's a kind of instinct,' he had told her, when they had wandered around various antique-shops, something that had utterly bored her, but that was in their first months of marriage. He liked small things. Articles she wouldn't be bothered to look at. He had tried to educate her when he had bought a gold George IV snuff-box. 'In a few years' time, this will be worth a lot more than I'm paying for it now.' She couldn't care less. Nor could she care less having thrown a valuable Chinese vase at him. Who cared for junk like that?

'Ah, coffee,' Lucan said and joined her at the table. 'Honey, you are one of the most beautiful women in the world.'

Sheila felt a rush of blood, and a driving sexual urge. 'Stay a while, Julian. Please don't go.'

He drank the coffee, still smiling at her.

'With the greatest regrets, I have to go.'

'When will you be back?'

'Not for a while. I will be busy all this week.'

Her heart sank.

'When can we meet again?'

37

He poured more coffee into his cup.

'We'll have to see. I don't often come this way.'

She felt a sudden uneasiness.

'But, Julian, don't you want . . .?' She paused, then stared at his smiling face.

'Oh, sure. I loved it, but I have to move around. Maybe I'll be your way in a month or so. Suppose I give you a call?'

'But, Julian . . .!'

'I said no way, honey.' She was aware that those sexy grey eyes were suddenly hard. 'And before I go, how about my stud-fee?'

She stared at him, her fists clenched on the table.

'What do you mean?'

His smile broadened.

'Be your age, honey. You don't imagine I spend a whole night with a woman without getting a fee, do you? It was good, wasn't it? You enjoyed it. So . . .'

'You mean you are asking me for money?' Sheila said, her voice a husky whisper.

'Let's settle for five hundred dollars,' Lucan said, his smile still wide, but his eyes now like chips of ice. 'For a full night, I usually charge a thousand, but seeing it is you . . .'

She sat for a long moment, motionless, then she jumped to her feet, her eyes flashing, her face contorted with fury.

'Get out!' she screamed at him. 'Get out or I'll call the police, you filthy blackmailer!'

Lucan shook his head sadly. He had been through this scene a number of times.

'That's a great idea, honey,' he said. 'Call the police. It'll be headline news tomorrow. Your husband and the guys he works with will love it. So will all your girl friends. Go ahead, call the cops.'

Sheila felt her fury drain out of her. God! What a fool she had been! She didn't care what Perry thought, but her friends mattered. Okay, most of them were having it off with each other's husbands, but, so far, they hadn't been caught. She could imagine the gossip. She wouldn't be able to show her face at the club again.

'Hurry it up, honey,' Lucan said, seeing her dismay. 'I've another baby with hot pants waiting.'

They stared at each other, then Lucan smiled.

'Well, you didn't perform badly. The dinner was good. Okay, this time I'll let you off the hook. There are times when I can be generous. When you get hot pants again, give me a call. You'll find me in the book. So long, baby, be seeing you,' and he walked from the room.

When she heard the front door slam, Sheila sank onto the settee.

God! What a crazy fool she had been! she thought. When her girl friends wanted a change in bed, they always picked on their friends' husbands. That way, there was security. To think she could have picked on a stranger! Her shame and fury was such, she burst into tears.

Ted Fleichman sat in his car opposite the Weston house. He held a Nikon camera fitted with an F 200 mm lens. He took three rapid shots of Lucan as he came out into the sunshine, then, dropping the camera on the passenger's seat, he swung out of the car and walked fast to where Lucan was opening the garage door.

Lucan, who was humming happily, only became aware of Fleichman when he felt a tap on his shoulder. Turning, he found Fleichman standing close to him.

'Hi, Lucky,' Fleichman said with his hard-cop grin. 'Had a good time?'

Lucan closed his hands into fists and scowled.

'Who the hell are you?' he demanded, not liking the cold tough eyes that were probing him.

'Security.' Fleichman produced his wallet and flashed a silver badge. 'Okay, no fuss, Lucky. Let's have it. The place is bugged. You could go away for ten. So hand it over.'

'I don't know what you're talking about,' Lucan said, his face paling under his tan.

'Don't let's waste time. You have another client waiting, so hand it over unless, of course, you want me to mess up your handsome face.'

'Hand what over?' Lucan demanded. 'What are you talking about?'

'Don't give me that crap, Lucky. She didn't give you any money, so you helped yourself to something. I know your methods. Come on, hand it over or I'll have to get rough with you.'

Lucan had had one or two unfortunate experiences with security guards. He realised to tangle with this thickset professional would lead to real trouble. He hesitated, then took from his pocket Perry's gold George IV snuff-box.

Fleichman produced a small plastic bag.

'Drop it in there, Lucky,' he said, 'then I'll have a nice set of your fingerprints. No tricks or I'll ruin your family jewels.'

Knowing Fleichman was capable of kneeing him in his most lucrative possession, Lucan dropped the snuff-box into the plastic bag.

'Okay, Lucky, now piss off. If you show your mug in my district again, you're for the cop house.'

Lucan glared at him, then got in his car and drove out of the garage and away.

Perry Weston came awake with a start. For a long moment, he didn't know where he was, then realised he was still sitting in the rented Toyota and the rain was hammering down still on the roof of the car.

He yawned and stretched. Too much Scotch, he thought, and looked at the clock on the dashboard. The time was 22.05. He'd better get moving. He turned on his headlights and looked at the highway road, dancing with rain. He should have stayed over at Jacksonville. He reckoned he was within ten miles of his fishing-lodge. A mile down the highway there was a turn-off that led to his destination, but the road could be bad. He opened the glove compartment, took out the bottle of Ballantine and took a long drink. Then replacing the bottle, he lit a cigarette and stared through the streaming windshield at the pelting rain.

Maybe he should have his head examined. To get to his fishing-lodge could be some performance, but the Scotch bolstered his determination.

He felt hungry. He hadn't been to the fishing-lodge for three years, but he had arranged with Mary Ross, the Sheriff's wife, to look in from time to time and keep an eye on the freezer.

He knew there was plenty of food in the freezer, and he knew Mary Ross had kept the lodge clean. He suddenly looked forward to seeing her again, and to having a beer with Sheriff Ross. They were both his kind of people and, in spite of his fame, they were real friendly.

He thought of Sheila. Okay, so she was having it off with men younger than himself. Silas S. Hart didn't make reckless statements. So what? Maybe when she got older she would settle down. He admitted to himself that it couldn't be great fun for her to be married to a man who worked long hours. Maybe, after this break, they could come together. Maybe . . .

He switched on the ignition and started the car's engine. Usually, the highway was crammed with trucks and cars, but it was now deserted.

Another ten miles to go. Take it slow, he said to himself. You're full of Scotch. Just take it slow.

He knew there would be a juicy steak waiting for him. He had an infra-red grill. In less than an hour, he would be sitting at the table, eating.

Ten miles to go!

He drove carefully along the highway. The windshield-wipers scarcely coped with the hammering rain, and he had to lean forward to peer into the wet darkness.

The turn-off couldn't now be far. He mustn't miss it. He slowed down to twenty-five miles an hour, then he saw a bright light flashing ahead of him. He slowed to a crawl. All he could see was the red light flashing and the wetness.

Some accident?

He stopped the car as the flashing red light moved towards him. Then the light of his headlights showed him a man wearing a rain-soaked Stetson hat and the yellow slicker of a Highway Patrol officer.

Jesus! he thought, if this guy smells my breath, I could be done for a drunk-driving rap.

He watched the man until he stepped out of the beams of the headlights. He pressed the button so the electrically driven driver's window sank. Rain pelted in the car and against his face. He waited, feeling the rain refreshing.

The man came alongside the car and flashed the red lamp at Perry. The beam moved to the passenger's seat, then to the back seats as if the man was checking that Perry was the only occupant in the car.

'What's the trouble?' Perry asked, seeing only the middle part of the man's body as the man stood close to the car.

'My car's run off the road.' The man bent slightly, but Perry could now only see the outline of the Stetson hat. 'I've got to get to a telephone. Where are you heading?'

'Rockville. I've a fishing-lodge two miles out of the village,' Perry said. 'You can use my phone.'

'Yeah.'

The man ran around the car. His wet slicker showed for a brief moment in the headlights. He opened the passenger's door and slid in beside Perry.

'Hell of a night,' Perry said as he shifted into gear.

'Yeah,' the man said. He had a hard clipped voice. 'Let's go.'

3

Hollis sat in Sheriff Ross's car and talked to Carl Jenner over the radio. He told Jenner that Deputy Sheriff Mason had just died.

For a moment, Jenner didn't seem able to grasp what Hollis was telling him, then he said, 'You mean this bastard killed young Mason?'

'Yes, sir. He's dead. He had a terrible blow on the head. I've found the weapon: an axe. All the others were killed in the same way. Their skulls were crushed like egg-shells. Mason only survived for a while because of his hat. This man must be as strong as an ox.'

'Good God!' Jenner exploded. 'Now six killings in one night! No one will be safe as long as this animal is free! Don't touch anything, Hollis. The homicide squad are trying to get to you. I've got cars covering Jacksonville. When Lewis and Johnson reach you, send them back to the highway. He could be heading for Miami. Tell them to head that way. The State police are trying to set up roadblocks, but in this rain it's a job.'

'Okay, sir,' Hollis said. 'I'll keep in touch,' and he switched off the radio.

A minute or so later, he saw headlights of an approaching car. The car pulled up beside him, and Lewis, the driver, leaned out of the window.

Shouting above the sound of the rain, Hollis gave him the picture.

'Orders are for you to belt back to the highway and head towards Miami fast. You just might overtake him. He's wearing a Stetson hat and a yellow slicker he took from

Mason,' Hollis bawled. 'He'll be in Mason's Ford. Number SZY 3002. Watch it! He has Mason's gun!'

'We hardly made it up this goddamn road,' Lewis moaned. 'It's like a quagmire. Okay, I'll do my best.'

'It'll have to be better than that!' Hollis snapped. 'This punk's got to be caught!'

After watching Lewis reverse his car, sliding in the mud, he ran back, through the rain to the shelter of the bungalow's lobby.

Sheriff Ross, looking ten years older, met Hollis as he came into the lobby.

'There's nothing for me to do here,' he said. 'I guess I'll get back to my office.'

Hollis felt sorry for him. The Sheriff looked a broken man.

'I need your radio, Sheriff,' he said. 'Please stay around until the ambulance comes, then drive down with them. Okay?'

'I wasn't thinking.' Ross walked heavily to an upright chair in the lobby and sat down. 'That boy was like a son to me. I can't believe he's dead.'

Hollis regarded him for a brief moment, then walked into the living-room.

Davis was leaning against the wall, smoking a cigarette, keeping his eyes from the three bodies.

'We don't touch a thing, Jerry,' Hollis said. 'The Homicide boys should be on their way. This killer could have left fingerprints, and he could have a record.'

'He's a real smart-ass,' Davis said. 'The big deal is to catch him. I'd hate to be the guy who corners him. He's got Mason's gun. Let's get out of here. This carnage turns my stomach.'

The two men joined the Sheriff in the lobby.

'You've got to get him,' Ross said, not looking up. 'The Loss family and Tom were my true friends. What's happening? What's Jenner doing?'

'There's a full State alert, Sheriff,' Hollis said. 'The State police are in on it. Tomorrow the National Guard will join in. Every motorist, if he's listening to his radio, is warned, but there can't be many motorists out on a night like this. There's not much else we can do tonight.'

'Okay, but this is for sure,' Ross looked up. There was a grim, determined expression on his white face. 'If you boys don't find him, I will, if it's the last thing I do.'

'Sure, Sheriff,' Hollis said, feeling for the old man. He thought this was kid's talk. By now the killer could be miles away, probably heading for Miami, far away from Ross's territory. 'Don't worry. Sooner or later, we'll find him.'

'I'll have to tell Tom's mother,' Ross muttered, and buried his face in his hands.

The rain continued to pelt down.

Perry Weston started the engine of the Toyota.

'Around a mile ahead, there's a turn-off to the left that leads to my place,' he said. 'God knows what the road'll be like. It's pretty rough even in dry weather.'

The man, sitting by his side, wearing a Stetson hat and a soaking wet slicker, said nothing.

'Would it be an idea for you to call for help on your radio?' Perry asked. 'All cop cars have radios, haven't they?'

'The radio's bust,' the man said.

'If it would be more helpful, I could take the branch road and you could telephone from the Sheriff's office.'

'Your phone is good as any.' The hard, metallic voice jarred on Perry.

'Well, okay.' Perry slowed the car. 'We're coming to the turn-off. It could be tricky.'

The man at his side said nothing.

One of those strong, silent, brainless types, Perry thought and shrugged.

He turned off the highway and onto a road that led, five miles ahead, to his fishing-lodge. The road was half tarmac, half sand.

Feeling he should make the offer, and now aware that the lodge would be dismal, he said, 'If you want to, you can stay the night. My place is well-organised, but maybe you want to get back to your car.'

45

There was a long pause.

'I don't give a damn about the car,' the man said. 'I'm off duty. I'll have to tell them where the car is. Sure, I'd like to spend the night. I've had it up to here with this rain.'

'Me too.' Perry leaned forward to stare at the narrow road scarcely lit by his headlights. 'Glad to have you. Who are you?'

'Keep driving, buster. Watch the road. It looks bad.'

Perry felt a sudden uneasiness. Although he couldn't take his eyes off the road, he wanted to look at this man by his side.

'We shouldn't be long,' he said. 'What's your name?'

Again there was a long pause.

'Call me Jim.'

'Jim – what?'

Again a pause.

'Brown.'

'Okay, Jim Brown. I'm Perry Weston.'

'Watch your driving,' the man who called himself Jim Brown snapped.

'Yeah. God! This rain!'

Jim Brown leaned forward, staring into the small pools of lights from the car's headlights. Suddenly he shouted, 'To your right!'

It was too late. A split second later, Perry saw a vast pool of rainwater and mud. The front wheels of the Toyota just managed to cross the pool, but the rear wheels sank. The car's engine stalled.

'Hell!' Perry exclaimed. 'We're stuck!'

'I told you to drive to the right,' the man beside him snapped.

'How the hell can anyone see anything in this rain!' Perry snapped back. 'We're stuck for good!'

'I think I can shift her. Let's take a look.'

The man slid out of the car and into the pelting rain. Cursing, Perry opened the driver's door and flinched as the rain beat down on him. He was wearing a light trench-coat that scarcely protected him as he floundered in the mud and the water.

46

Brown was already standing up to his ankles in the pool. He turned on his flashlight, grunted, then looked towards where Perry was standing.

'I can get her out,' he said.

'How do I help?' Perry asked, feeling helpless.

'I'll handle it. Get in the car, start the engine and , when I yell, move into gear and creep forward. Understand?'

Perry stared with amazement as the man turned his back to the car and caught hold of the rear bumper in his gloved hands.

'You'll never shift her,' he exclaimed. 'Let me help.'

'Get in the car and do what I've told you!' the man barked. 'I'll shift the sonofabitch!'

Crazy! Perry thought. To try and lift the Toyota, loaded with luggage, out of this quagmire!

'Suppose we both . . .' he began.

'Will you goddamn do what I tell you!' The voice was a hard bark that startled Perry.

'Well, okay.' He was glad to climb into the shelter of the car. He started the engine.

'Now!' the man yelled.

Perry shifted into gear and gently pressed the accelerator. He felt the back of the car lift, the wheels spun, then gripped tarmac and rolled forward.

Perry could scarcely believe it. The car was again on firm ground! He slightly accelerated and the car moved forward, then he trod on the brake.

He had imagined he would have had to walk to his fishing-lodge, leaving his car bogged down, and would have to telephone for someone to pull the car out of the quagmire. This man had actually lifted the rear end of the car and had shoved it forward on its front wheels, doing the work of a breakdown truck! Incredible!

He must be as strong as an ox, Perry thought, unaware he was using the same phrase as Hollis had used when talking to Jenner on the radio about the savage murders.

Brown appeared, his head bent against the rain at Perry's window.

'We're clear,' he said. 'Shift over. I'll do the driving.'

'I know the road. You don't,' Perry said. 'I'd better drive.'

'Shift over!' The man jerked open the door and shoved himself in as Perry was forced to move into the passenger's seat.

As the man set the car moving, Perry realised he was thankful he didn't have to drive. He felt, if anyone could get them down to the lodge, this man could. He reached into the glove compartment and produced the bottle of Scotch.

'Have a drink, Jim.'

'I don't drink.'

Perry unscrewed the cap on the bottle and took a long swig.

'Well, have a cigarette.'

'I don't smoke.'

Perry blew out his cheeks and shrugged. He replaced the bottle in the glove compartment, then sat back, staring into the darkness and the pelting rain.

'We have around three miles to go,' he said. 'Man! Will I be glad to get home!'

Brown kept silent. He drove with skill and confidence, watching the road, following the twists and bends.

Perry was now able to look at him, but the light from the dashboard revealed little. He saw brown, big hands on the steering-wheel; the outline of the Stetson hat, but nothing of the man's face.

Curious to know more about this man, he asked, 'Have you been long with the highway patrol?'

A long pause, then Brown said, 'Long enough.'

'That's a good answer. I'm always saying that about my job. I write film scripts.' Perry eased himself against the back of the seat. 'You married?'

'No.'

'To have shifted this car the way you did, you must be a weight-lifter in your spare time.'

Brown said nothing.

The condition of the road was improving and Brown increased speed.

'Do you go to the movies? You might have seen one of my films,' Perry said. 'Ever seen *The Gun Duel*? That was one of mine.'

'I don't go to the movies.'

Man! Perry thought. This guy is a real square. He doesn't drink, smoke nor go to the movies. What the hell does he do? He asked the question, 'So what do you do in your spare time except police work?'

'Stop flapping with your mouth!' There was a snarl in Brown's voice. 'I'm driving!'

'Okay . . . sorry,' Perry said. He lit a cigarette and resisted taking another drink.

They drove for the next twenty minutes in silence, then Perry said, 'Take the turn to the right, and we're there.'

When they finally reached the fishing-lodge and Brown drove into the garage, Perry heaved a sigh of relief. He knew he couldn't have made it, but, somehow, this man had coaxed the car through the mud with an expertise that baffled Perry. He was sure, if he had been driving, he would have been bogged down a number of times, but they were under shelter at last.

'That was great driving, Jim!' he said as they both got out of the car. 'You certainly did a fine job.'

Brown moved to the entrance of the garage and peered out into the darkness and the pelting rain. Perry groped and found the light-switch and turned on the light.

'Let's dump our wet things here. No point in messing up my place,' he said, and stripped off his soaking trench-coat. He dragged off his boots.

The man came away from the entrance of the garage and pulled off his mud-encrusted boots. Then the Stetson hat came off, then the yellow slicker.

In the light reflecting down on him, Perry could now see him clearly.

What he saw gave him a jolt of uneasiness. The man was about his own height, but his shoulders were broader. At first glance he looked like a primitive rock carving: long arms, a chunky body, long legs and the power and muscular build was awe-inspiring.

Then the face: ice-cold blue eyes, a short, blunt nose, high cheek-bones and thick lips as if fashioned in red putty. The hair was the colour of straw and cut in a fringe across a low forehead, dirty and shoulder-length.

Perry saw around this man's thick waist was a revolver belt, and in the holster a gun butt showed.

A real character, Perry thought. Straight from the apes.

'Let's get some comfort,' he said, wondering why a high-way patrol officer should be wearing a dirty white sweat-shirt and black jeans. He shrugged this thought off as he groped for his keys and unlocked the door leading straight into his living-room. 'Come on in, Jim.' He turned on the lights and led the way into the big room. 'Maybe you'll want to get out of those clothes. I can fix you up. Man! Is it good to get out of that goddamn rain!'

Brown was staring around the big, comfortably fur-nished room. For some seconds the luxury of what he was seeing seemed to stun him.

Finally, he muttered, 'You live pretty well.'

'It's okay. How about a bath? I'm taking one, then I'll organise a meal. I'll find something for you to wear. I'll show you your room.' As he moved towards the stairs, he paused. 'I was forgetting. You want to telephone. The phone's over there.'

'It'll wait,' Brown said. 'I want to get out of these wet things.'

Shrugging, Perry led the way up the stairs.

'Your room's the second on the left,' he said. 'I'll find you something to wear.'

He entered the major bedroom and turned on the lights. He looked at the big double bed which he had hoped to have shared with Sheila, but in spite of his efforts to per-suade her she had refused to come to the fishing-lodge. He paused, for a long moment, thinking of her. What was she doing right now? He glanced at his watch. The time was well after midnight. Then grimacing, he went to his big closet, found a sweat-shirt, underpants and a pair of jeans. These he carried down the short corridor and entered the second bedroom.

Brown was standing by the bed, staring around the room.

'Here you are. I think you can squeeze into them,' Perry said, tossing the clothes on the bed. 'Me for a bath. See you in half an hour.'

'This is pretty fancy,' Brown said, still staring around the room.

'Glad you like it. The bathroom's right there,' Perry said, longing to get out of his damp clothes and into a hot bath. He left the room and entered his bedroom.

As he drew water in the bath, he wondered about the weather conditions. Was this rain going to cease? Stripping, he took his small transistor radio with him into the bathroom and put it on a shelf by the bath. He turned it on, then sank, with a sigh of pleasure, into the hot water.

He was in time to catch the weather forecast. Rain was expected to persist for the next twenty-four hours, but would gradually die out, giving way to a spell of hot, humid weather.

Perry shrugged.

He knew he had plenty of food in the freezer. In a couple of days, with luck, he could start fishing and thinking. He grimaced, wondering if some idea would come to him. It was odd how ideas for a plot could develop in a hot bath. He thought of Silas S. Hart and what he wanted: sex, blood and action. There was time. After all, he had only just arrived. He was hungry. As he got out of the bath and reached for a towel, the impersonal voice of the radio announcer said: *'We are interrupting this programme for an urgent police message. All motorists travelling between Jacksonville and Miami are warned . . .'*

Perry snapped off the transistor. He was now no longer a motorist. He was home, dry and hungry. Let the other poor sods floundering in the rain, listen to police warnings. So he didn't hear the warning that a man, now called the Axe Killer, was at large and disguised as a highway patrol officer.

All Perry could think of right now was a thick, juicy steak. Hastily drying himself, he scrambled into a sweat-

51

shirt, jeans and loafers and ran down the stairs to the living-room.

He found Brown moving around the room aimlessly. Perry paused in the doorway. Brown had taken a bath. His straw-coloured hair was clean and lay flat against his skull. He had squeezed himself into Perry's clothes. The short-sleeved sweat-shirt was too small and revealed this man's bulging muscles. Perry saw on this man's left, thick forearm the tattoo of a striking cobra snake. Around his solid waist was the cartridge belt and gun.

Man! Perry thought. This guy is certainly a character!

'Hungry!' he asked, moving into the room. 'I'm starving. How about a steak?'

'Not for me,' Brown said. 'I guess I'll take a kip, but you go ahead, buster.'

Perry suddenly realised he was beginning to dislike this man. He now regretted offering him a bed, but what else could he have done? Maybe he should have driven him to the Sheriff's office and have got rid of him.

'Cut out calling me buster,' he said sharply. 'I told you my name's Perry Weston . . . okay?'

Brown stared at him for a long moment. His ice-blue eyes were intimidating. Then he shrugged.

'Sure. I'll catch up on sleep.'

'You wanted to use the telephone,' Perry said, thinking that there might be a chance for a highway patrol car to come and pick this man up and he would be rid of him.

'Yeah. Right.' Brown moved slowly towards him. 'The phone's out of order. My fault.' He gave a short, barking laugh. 'I guess I don't know my own strength.'

The sound of that mirthless laugh sent a cold prickle down Perry's spine.

'I'm not with you,' he said. 'What's the matter with the phone?'

'Bust,' Brown said, still moving forward. Perry stepped aside. 'Don't worry about it. Have your steak. I'm taking a kip.'

Perry watched Brown walk into the lobby and then climb the stairs. He went quickly to the telephone and saw the cable was dangling. It had been wrenched out of its socket.

He heard a door upstairs slam shut.

He stood thinking. Something was very wrong. This man just could not be a highway patrol officer: not with his long hair and the clothes he had been wearing. Then who was he? What the hell have I got myself into? he asked himself. Then he remembered there had been a police warning which he hadn't bothered to listen to. Had that warning been anything to do with this man? Maybe there would be other warnings.

He no longer felt hungry. He had to admit he was now more than uneasy. Maybe the warning would be repeated on the television. He crossed to the set, then paused, seeing the cable dangling. That too had been wrenched out of the socket and the plug was missing. Shocked, he remained motionless, aware his heart was thumping, then he remembered the transistor he had left in his bathroom.

Moving silently, he climbed the stairs, entered his bedroom and moved into the bathroom, switching on the light. One quick glance told him the transistor was no longer there.

Jesus! he thought, this is becoming really something! Then he remembered the radio in the Toyota. Again moving silently, he crept down the stairs. Reaching the door that let into the garage, he turned the handle to find the door locked and the key missing.

So he was cut off, isolated, alone with this ape of a man! No outside help!

Controlling a rising panic, he walked slowly back into the living-room. He poured himself a stiff Scotch and drank it neat. Then he refilled his glass and sat down in one of the big lounging chairs.

Some situation, he thought. He was now convinced this man, up in the spare bedroom, was dangerous, possibly crazy. He had a gun. Apart from the gun, he was horrifyingly strong.

Perry emptied his glass, then placed the glass carefully

on the occasional table, so carefully the glass fell to the floor.

Perry closed his eyes. So, okay, he was smashed. He hadn't eaten for ten hours. He had been drinking steadily since he had got on the plane. So, okay, he was smashed.

He stretched out his long legs and made himself comfortable.

Some situation! Could this turn into the script that Silas S. Hart was demanding. Blood, sex and action?

Who cares? he muttered. Who cares about a guy with a gun? Who the hell cares about anything?

Lulled by the sound of the rain and the moaning of the wind in the trees, Perry Weston passed out.

Sheriff Ross sat at his desk listening to Carl Jenner on the telephone. The time was 03.00, and Ross was feeling bone-weary and utterly depressed. He had ridden back in the ambulance which contained four brutally murdered bodies. He had sat beside Dr O'Leary, Jacksonville's medical examiner: a short, thickset man in his late fifties.

'Never seen anything like this,' O'Leary muttered.

Ross said nothing. He was thinking of Tom Mason; his mother would have to be told, and his friends who had been friends of his for the past fifteen years.

The ambulance driver had dropped Ross outside his office. With a brief word of thanks and a nod to O'Leary, Ross entered his office. As he stripped off his soaking wet slicker and hat, he told his wife what had happened.

'It's a terrible thing,' he said, walking to his desk and sitting down. 'I'll have to tell Tom's mother.'

'Tomorrow will do. Let the poor soul have her night's rest,' Mary said. 'Now don't worry about it. I'll tell her. I have coffee for you. Why don't you get some sleep?'

'I want to talk to Jenner,' Ross said, reaching for the telephone. 'I've got to know what's going on. The State police have taken over, but that doesn't mean I can go to bed!'

'Jeff! This dreadful thing has now nothing to do with you,' Mary said gently. 'It's all in good hands. Now, come to bed.'

Ross was already talking to Jenner.

'Yeah, but nothing helpful,' Jenner told him. 'Mason's car was found tipped into a ditch around twenty-five miles from the farm on the highway. Jacklin, who is now in charge of the investigation, thinks the killer must have stopped a passing motorist and got a lift, posing as a highway patrol officer. Radio warnings are out. Any motorist giving a patrol officer a lift is asked to contact headquarters. So far, nothing. Jacklin thinks he could be by now in Miami. The Homicide squad turned up nothing. The killer didn't leave fingerprints: must have worn gloves. The murder weapon is clean. We have a description of him, but it's vague. I haven't had time to tell you the details, but here's what happened. A motorcycle patrol officer spotted a hold-up at a garage. He sent a radio that he was making an arrest. A patrol car, picking up the message, was in time to find the hold-up man trying to start the police motorcycle. The officer who radioed was dead, and the gas attendant so badly wounded he also died. The two patrol officers tackled the killer. Sergeant Hurst was badly wounded, but Trooper Brownlow clubbed the man unconscious. Brownlow is new to this racket. He searched the unconscious man and found a driver's licence made out in the name of Chet Logan. He threw the man into the back of the car, then attended to Hurst, who was bleeding badly. I guess Brownlow lost his head. All he could think of was to get Hurst to hospital. He forgot to put handcuffs on the unconscious killer. Can you imagine? He drove fast to Abbeville. The road conditions were bad. He did have the sense to report to me on the radio as he was driving. From what Brownlow told me we have a vague description of the man. You already have that. The big thing is this man has a cobra snake tattooed on his left arm. I guess Brownlow, while talking to me, must have taken his eyes off the road. I heard the crash over the radio. He and Hurst were dead by the time we found them, and Logan had vanished. That's it, Jeff. Captain Jacklin has now taken charge. This is a State police job. There's nothing either you or me can do. This killer could be miles away by now and off our neck of the woods.'

'The killing took place on my territory,' Ross snapped. 'How does Jacklin know this man is heading for Miami? He could have doubled back. Along the river there are a number of fishing-lodges. Most of them are shut. He could be hiding in one of those. He could be hiding any place on my ground. As soon as this goddamn rain lets up, I'm going to check. If I find him, if it's the last thing I do, I'll make him pay for killing Tom and my friends!'

'I can't stop you,' Jenner said, restraining his impatience. 'This man must be running to Miami where he can get lost. But okay, suppose he has doubled back? You start checking out likely hiding-places, and you'll land up with a bullet in your head. This man is vicious and armed. Tomorrow there'll be a massive search within twenty miles of where Mason's car was found. Jacklin has called out the National Guard. You keep out of it, Jeff.'

'The National Guard don't know the ground as I do,' Ross said.

'I'll tell Jacklin to consult you. Now, for God's sake, don't start acting like a hero, Jeff. You'll need another deputy. Sergeant Hank Hollis is due promotion. He's a good man. Okay, with you?'

'Sure. I know Hank. He's a good man.'

'Right. He'll report to you tomorrow morning. Now go to bed. If this rain continues, and the forecasters say it will, tomorrow is going to be a very tough day.'

'In the meantime, this killer is loose.'

'But not for long, Jeff. Good-night,' and Jenner hung up.

Having watched Julian Lucan drive away, Ted Fleichman returned to his car. He took off the cassette that recorded from the bug in the Weston house and dropped it into his pocket. He lit a cigarette and stared into space, his mind active.

He knew Perry Weston was a rich man. Although Fleichman's salary, working as a private investigator, was good, he was in the hole for ten thousand dollars. His wife was never out of a doctor's hands. She was never out of a dentist's hands. Well, okay, some women were like that. He loved his wife, who was five years older than himself, but the bills that kept coming in weighed on him. The last check he had on what he now owed came to $9,800, and he had had firm letters asking for payment.

He would have to find the money. He rubbed his jaw while he thought of Perry Weston. Ten thousand dollars would be peanuts to a man in his earning bracket.

This would have to be handled carefully, he told himself, but he could swing a deal. Weston was out of town. Maybe the wife could produce ten thousand dollars.

It was worth a careful try.

Sheila Weston had got over her crying jag. An experience! she told herself. Never again! No more strangers! She was young enough to be resilient. Today was Sunday, and she was alone. She decided she would go to the tennis club and have lunch. Julian Lucan was already fading into her past. A marvellous sexy lover! She suddenly smiled. She certainly had handled him beautifully. He had given her the sex thrill of her life, and it had cost her nothing! But never again! She would take a shower, dress for tennis and spend the rest of the day at the club.

As she walked into the lobby, heading for the stairs, the front door-bell rang.

Who could this be? she wondered, frowning, aware she was only wearing a wrap over her nakedness, then with an impatient shrug she went to the door and opened it.

She was confronted by a thickset man, wearing a dark light-weight suit, white shirt and a white linen cap with a long peak.

'Morning, Mrs Weston,' the man said with a wide smile. 'Sorry to disturb you. I'm Ted Fleichman, Acme Investigations.' He produced a wallet and flashed a silver badge. 'Security, madam.'

'I am not interested,' Sheila snapped. 'Thank you,' and began to shut the door.

Fleichman, still smiling, shoved his foot forward so the door wouldn't close.

'You and me, Mrs Weston, need to talk. It's to do with

Julian Lucan, the man who spent the night with you.'

The shock of hearing this was so great Sheila felt her heart skip a beat and felt blood drain out of her face. She took two unsteady steps backwards, allowing Fleichman to move into the lobby. He closed the front door.

'Go away!' Sheila said, her voice a whisper. 'You've no right to come in here! Go away!'

Fleichman's smile broadened.

'Sure, no problem, Mrs Weston. I'll go away if that's what you want, but I could help you. I want to help you. It's part of my job. You see, I've been hired to watch you. I have to turn in a report, but if you want me to go away that's just what I'll have to do.'

'Watch me? Who has hired you? My husband?' Sheila was now recovering. This tough-looking man seemed friendly. Could Perry have done such a thing . . . to have her watched?

'No, madam,' Fleichman said. 'Nothing to do with Mr Weston. Sorry, I can't name my client. Can't we sit down and talk about this?'

'No! Go away!'

'Okay, madam. Anything you say. I just wanted to help you, but if you want me to turn in my report that you spent the night with Lucky Lucan, you have only to say so.'

'No one will believe you!' Sheila cried desperately. 'You're just a spy! You have no proof! Now get out!'

'Proof!' Fleichman shook his head. 'If you mean there's no evidence, madam, I have to correct you. I have a recording of what happened last night, and what happened this morning. I have photographs of Lucan leaving here. You probably haven't had time to look around to see if anything is missing. Lucan always gets paid: either in cash or a present.' He took from his pocket the plastic bag containing the gold George IV snuff-box and dangled it so Sheila could see it. 'I believe this is your property, madam. I persuaded Lucan to give it to me.'

Not believing what she was seeing, Sheila ran into the living-room and to the table where Perry's antique collection was displayed. She saw at once the snuff-box was missing.

Fleichman had moved into the living-room and stood watching her.

'Give it to me! It belongs to my husband!' Sheila exclaimed.

Fleichman looked sad.

'I wish I could, madam, but it has Lucan's finger-prints on it. His prints establish the fact that he stole it. The tape I have establishes the fact that he tried to extort five hundred dollars from you which you rightly refused to give him. The combination of his prints, the tape and the photographs will put him in the slammer for at least five years. It is my duty to hand the evidence to the NYC police. They have been waiting to get their hands on him, but, up to now, he's been too smart.'

Sheila felt her knees buckling. She sat down, staring at Fleichman, who also sat down, opposite her.

'You see what I mean, madam. It's a problem,' he said.

Sheila shuddered.

Awful thoughts flashed through her mind. A police enquiry! She would be called as a witness. Her friends! The sniggers and the whispers! Her social life, which she loved, ruined! God! What a lunatic fool she had been!

'This is a shock to you, madam?' Fleichman said. 'Should I get you a drink?' He looked around, saw the liquor cabinet, got up and poured a generous shot of Cognac into a glass. He took the drink to her. 'Come along, madam. Drink it.'

With a shaking hand, Sheila took the glass and swallowed the brandy in one quick gulp. She shuddered and let Fleichman take the glass from her. He returned to his chair and sat down.

For several minutes, Sheila sat motionless. The Cognac began to knit her together. Her mind began to work.

'As I have said, madam,' Fleichman said, seeing she was recovering from the shock, his voice gentle, 'there is a problem . . . for you and for me.'

She looked up and stared at him.

'For you?'

'Yes, madam. I have as big a problem as you have.'

'I don't understand. What is your problem?'

'Well, madam, unlike you, I have a financial problem. I am being paid to keep tabs on you. I've been keeping tabs on you for the past two months. I know you have been having fun with certain men. I know who they are. I know Mr Weston has been busy and perhaps neglectful. What is more natural for a young, attractive woman like you to have sex from time to time with other men? It happens every day. I know you have been with two of your men friends at various motels, but this time you fell for a professional, and you invited him to your home. That, madam, was a fatal mistake.'

Sheila stiffened.

'Who is employing you?'

'I can't give you the name of my client, madam. That would be a breach of confidence. When I investigate a woman who is playing around, it's my job to investigate in depth. I have learned you and Mr Weston have drifted apart. Divorce evidence wouldn't worry you, but for the police and the press to know that you have been foolish enough to take on a professional . . .' He paused to stare at her as he saw her flinch. 'Well, I don't have to spell it out, do I?'

Sheila's hands closed into fists.

'What is your problem?' she asked.

'I have a sick wife, madam,' Fleichman said, crossing one thick leg over the other. 'I won't bore you with the details. I don't earn much and the medical bills are more than I can pay. I am in debt, madam. I need ten thousand dollars. Now, madam, the NYC police want Lucan. They know private investigators like me often watch Lucan.' Fleichman paused, then went on, lying smoothly, 'They are offering any investigator who can produce strong enough evidence to put Lucan behind bars ten thousand dollars.'

The lie, to Sheila, was so obvious, she closed her eyes. To be blackmailed twice in a morning was something she couldn't believe possible.

'You see, madam,' Fleichman went on, 'I have to think of my wife, but I have also to think of you. I realise your nice life will be spoilt if you are forced to give evidence against Lucan. It is not as if you are one of many thousands of women who have fun on the side. You are the wife of a very famous script-writer. The press will have a ball if Lucan comes up for trial.' He paused, smiling sadly. 'I suggest you are not without money. I leave it to you. I must have ten thousand dollars. I know the police will willingly give it to me, but if you give it to me I will hand over the tape, the snuff-box and the photographs and you'll hear no more of this unfortunate affair. I will, of course, have to continue to watch you, but I assure you, in the future, if you step out of turn, I won't report it. In fact, madam, you will have gained a friend.' He gave her a big, friendly smile. 'Do we have a deal, madam?'

Sheila sat silent, looking down at her hands, gripped between her knees.

Fleichman waited. He was sure she would give him the money. Time meant nothing to him, but after minutes had ticked by he said, a sharper note in his voice, 'Do we have a deal, madam?'

'I don't seem to have any alternative, do I?' Sheila said in a hard cold voice. She didn't look up. 'I haven't such a sum, but my husband might have it in his safe upstairs. I'll see. Wait here.'

Still not looking at him, she got to her feet and walked out of the room. Moving like a shadow, Fleichman left his chair and moved to the living-room door. He watched Sheila climb the stairs and disappear into a room down a short corridor. Silently, he ran up the stairs and peered into the room.

Her back to him, Sheila was taking a modern painting off the wall. He saw the painting had concealed a small wall safe, and he grinned. He hadn't thought it would be this easy, but then, after all, she was only a kid, and he had scared her witless.

As Sheila began to turn the combination knob, the telephone bell rang. She turned, then saw Fleichman standing

61

in the doorway. She stifled a scream, her hand flying to her mouth.

'Don't answer it, madam,' Fleichman said, moving further into the room. 'Just open the safe.'

She moved so swiftly, he had no time to stop her. She snatched up the telephone receiver as he caught hold of her wrist, but she said loudly, 'Sheila here. Who is it?'

Fleichman released her wrist.

'Watch what you say!' he said, in a low snarling voice.

'Sheila, honey, it's Mavis.'

'Oh . . . Mavis,' Sheila made an effort to steady her voice.

'I couldn't wait. Has that gorgeous hunk of man left or is he still with you?'

'He's left.'

'Was he good?'

'So-so.'

'Honey, you sound flat. He looked marvellous!'

'Yes.'

'I must tell you. Sam turned up last night without warning. What a lucky escape I had! I was about to go out with Lew! Can you imagine? I'm almost a ruin. Right now, Sam's snoring his head off. The way he went on, you would have thought he hadn't screwed a woman for thirty years.'

'Well, that's Sam.'

'You can say that again. Heard from Perry?'

'No. He's on location somewhere in California.'

'California? He can't be, honey. He's in Florida. Sam saw him at the Jacksonville airport.'

'I thought he was in California,' Sheila said, aware of Fleichman.

'He's probably cheating on you, baby. You coming to the club? Sam will sleep all afternoon.'

'Maybe. I must go, Mavis. My bath is running. 'Bye for now,' and she hung up.

'If the phone rings again, madam,' Fleichman snapped, 'you don't answer it. Get that safe open!'

He stood back and watched her walk to the safe.

Ten thousand dollars! he thought. Man! Would that get him out of deep trouble! A guy like Perry Weston was certain to have a load of money in a wall safe. Maybe he should have asked for more. There would be further doctors' bills. He had this kid where he wanted her. Maybe he had better take a look, seeing she had now opened the safe door. As he moved forward, he stopped short.

Sheila had spun around. She was holding a vicious-looking .38 revolver in her hand which she had snatched from the safe.

In spite of his toughness, Fleichman felt a sudden chill as he stared first at the gun, then at Sheila's hard, desperate face.

'Put the snuff-box and the tape on that table,' she said. 'I can shoot! I'll smash your kneecap and you'll be crippled for life! Do what I say!'

Fleichman forced an uneasy grin.

'That gun ain't loaded,' he said. 'You don't bluff me,' and he edged forward.

There was a bang of gunfire. He felt something like a hornet whizz past his face. He started back. He had never been faced with an experience like this, and his sagging confidence oozed out of him.

'Okay . . . okay.' He took the tape and the plastic bag from his pocket and put them on the bedside table.

'Now, get out, you filthy blackmailer!' Sheila screamed at him. 'Get out!'

She followed him down the stairs, watched him open the front door and walk unsteadily down the drive. She slammed the door shut and shot the bolt.

Then she collapsed in a faint on the floor.

4

On this Sunday morning at 10.15, a police car pulled up outside Sheriff Ross's office.

Captain Fred Jacklin heaved his bulk out of the car, slammed the door and ran up the wooden steps to the porch out of the rain that cascaded down. If anything, he thought, taking off his soaked slicker, the rain was heavier than the previous day.

Jacklin was a massively built man with rugged features and the cold grey eyes of a cop. Head of the Jacksonville's State police department, nudging forty-eight years of age, he was known as an efficient and ruthless police officer.

He shook his slicker free of water, then walked into the office to find Sheriff Ross and Hank Hollis bending over a large-scale map spread out on Ross's desk.

'Hi, Jeff,' Jacklin said, advancing. 'Looks as if this rain's going to continue.'

The two men shook hands, and Jacklin nodded to Hollis.

'That's the way it looks, Captain,' Ross said. 'What's the news?'

'If you mean have we found this killer, the answer is no,' Jacklin said. 'He could be anywhere by now. All we can do in this rain is to keep broadcasting.' He pulled up a straight-backed chair and straddled it. 'Roadblocks have been set up, but it took time and he could have slipped through. No motorist has reported giving him a lift. In fact, we are getting nothing from our radio warnings. He could have stopped a motorist while wearing the patrol's uniform, killed him and taken off in the victim's car. This man will stop at nothing. I've turned out the National Guard. They are sitting in their trucks waiting for the rain to stop. So right now, we are getting nowhere.'

Ross went around his desk and sat down. He looked pale and tired.

'This is the map of my territory,' he said, tapping the map spread out on his desk. 'What you say makes sense, but there were very few motorists on the highway last night. I have a hunch that when Logan slid off the road and into a ditch, he took to the forest on foot. I think he could still be on my territory.'

Jacklin nodded.

'It's a possibility, but he must know that the roads are now sealed off, and once in the forest, he wouldn't have a chance to break out. No, Jeff. I still think he hijacked a car, killed the driver and is heading for Miami where he could get lost.'

'I know this territory like the back of my hand.' Ross tapped the map. 'There are dozens of places where this man could hide, but the places I like most are the fishing-lodges along the river.' He pointed to the map. 'They are less than ten miles from where he ditched Tom's car. There are footpaths through the forest that lead to the river. Now these fishing-lodges are unoccupied. They are only used from time to time by people from Miami, from New York. If this man could find one of these places, he'd have no trouble breaking in. I know the owners leave food in their freezers. He could remain in hiding in one of these lodges for two or three weeks while your men hunt for him. These fishing-lodges must be checked.'

Jacklin grunted. He wasn't convinced.

'It's an idea. What do you suggest?'

'I'm going to check them out,' Ross said. 'As soon as this rain lessens, Hank and I are going.'

'Now, hold it!' Jacklin said sharply. 'You two could get your heads blown off. This man has already killed six people! He's as dangerous as a cornered tiger, and he has Mason's gun. You keep out of it, Jeff!'

'This is my territory,' Ross said quietly. 'If he's hiding in the forest or in one of the fishing-lodges, I'll find him.'

Jacklin shrugged, then smiled.

'You're a stubborn old bastard, Jeff. Okay. I'll send four of the National Guards to you. I want you to take them with you.' He got to his feet. 'This rain will last another six or seven hours. I've got to get back to Jenner. I still think, by now, he's in Miami, but if he's still around here, you'll need support.'

He shook hands and ran out to his car.

Ross snorted.

'The National Guard! What good are they: goddamn kids with rifles!'

'Yeah. They could get in the way,' Hollis said. 'We can do without them.'

Ross regarded Hollis thoughtfully. Although he grieved that Tom Mason was dead, looking at Hollis, he could see this tall, lean man with his steady grey-blue eyes and his hard, firm mouth was infinitely superior to Mason. This man had years of experience as a highway patrol officer. He had also served in Vietnam. Ross was thankful to have him as his deputy.

Hollis walked to the window and looked out at the rain. Rockville's main street was deserted. He shrugged and turned to see Ross staring down at the map on his desk.

'Hank, I've got to get this man,' Ross said in a low voice. 'He killed my deputy and three of my friends. I can't sit around here waiting for the rain to stop.' He looked up and stared at Hollis. 'Feel like getting wet?'

Hollis grinned.

'I was hoping you'd say that, Sheriff.'

Ross nodded.

'Take a look at this map. We can drive to this point here.' He pointed to the map. 'Here, there is a footpath that leads down to the river. It's a good two-mile walk. There are five fishing-lodges along the river. They are around half a mile apart. This is going to take time, Hank, but if he's anywhere on my ground he'll be in one of these lodges. What do you say?'

'I'm with you, Sheriff.'

'Okay. We could be out all day. Mary's with Tom's mother. I'll leave her a note.' Ross went to the gun rack, unlocked it and took out two rifles. He then went to his desk and found a box of ammunition. 'You load up, Hank. I'll write a note to Mary,' and he sat down at his desk.

The note written, he went into the kitchen and cut four thick ham sandwiches which he put in a plastic bag, then he returned to his office to find Hollis, guns under his arm, wearing his slicker and hat, waiting.

'I'll call Jenner,' Ross said. 'I don't want him to try to contact me and get no answer.' Picking up the telephone receiver, he dialled.

When Jenner came on the line, Ross said, 'This is Jeff. I'm closing the office, Carl. I'm taking a look at the fishing-lodges. Could take me all day.'

'You're crazy!' Jenner snapped. 'You'll never get down to the river. Anyway, I . . .'

'This line's terrible,' Ross said. 'I just wanted you to know,' and he hung up.

At Ross's nod, Hollis ran out to the patrol car and slid under the steering-wheel. Ross paused long enough to lock the office door, then he joined him.

'Let's go,' he said.

With the windshield-wipers scarcely coping with the pelting rain, Hollis drove down Rockville's main street and headed for the highway.

Perry Weston came out of a sodden sleep like a man crawling out of quicksand. He looked around the big bedroom, only half focussing, then he shut his eyes and groaned.

He became aware of the sound of rain slamming against the windows, and he groaned again.

What a dope he had been to have come down here, he thought. What a dope to have paid no attention to the Hertz girl who had warned him that the rain was going to be bad.

For some minutes, he lay still before his mind began to function. He vaguely remembered staggering up the stairs and dropping onto his bed. That seemed years ago. He found he was still wearing the sweat-shirt and jeans, but he had kicked off his shoes.

Then into his mind floated an unpleasant vision of a powerfully built man with a cobra snake tattooed on his arm. Jim Brown!

Abruptly, he swung his legs off the bed and sat up.

How long had he slept? He looked at his strap watch. The time was 11.20.

Had the man gone?

Slowly, he dragged himself to his feet and went to the bedroom door. He opened it, and stood listening. He heard movements downstairs. He could smell coffee.

So Jim Brown was still here!

He shut the door and moved into the bathroom. He paused to look at himself in the mirror. What a goddamn wreck! he thought. He should never have hit the bottle as he had done the previous night.

Making an effort, he shaved, then stripping off, he stood under a cold-water shower. By the time he had dried himself, he was feeling a lot better.

Going to the closet, he put on a short-sleeved shirt and a pair of linen slacks.

While he was shaving, showering and dressing, he was thinking of Jim Brown.

This man, he decided, was either a nut-case or a fugitive. Whoever he was, he was dangerous. With the telephone dead, the rain hammering down, locked out from his car, there was nothing he could do except play this one off the cuff. He had no alternative.

Bracing himself, he left the bedroom and walked down the stairs. He paused in the lobby. The smell of coffee was now added to the sound of meat sizzling.

He pushed open the kitchen door and then paused.

Brown was standing over the infra-red grill. His head jerked around and the two men stared at each other.

Brown was wearing the clothes Perry had given him. Around his waist was the gun-belt. His thick lips parted in a grin.

'How's about a steak, buster?' he said. 'You've got good

food in the freezer. Won't take five minutes. Okay?'

'Fine,' Perry said. 'I can't remember when I ate last.'

Brown turned back to the grill.

'I've made a pot of coffee. Suppose you go in there and sit, huh? Give me five minutes.'

Accepting the situation, Perry walked into the living-room. He found the dining-table laid. This man had found the cutlery, the salt, pepper and mustard. He realised how hungry he was. He was tempted to go to the liquor-cabinet and pour himself a shot of Scotch, but resisted the tempta-tion. Instead, he walked to the big window and, pushing aside the curtain, looked out at the rain, the mud and the dripping trees.

Play this off the cuff, he thought. There's nothing I can do about it. This man holds all the cards.

He moved restlessly around the room until Brown came in, carrying a tray. He put down two plates, loaded with perfectly cooked steaks, peas and fried potatoes.

'Here we go,' he said. 'You have a fancy setup here.'

They sat opposite each other and began to eat.

This man could cook, Perry thought. The steaks were excellent. Halfway through the silent meal, Brown paused and looked at Perry.

'Buster, I'm sorry about this. I'm really sorry.'

Play it off the cuff, Perry told himself. He cut off a piece of steak, smothered it with mustard, then before convey-ing it to his mouth, he asked quietly, 'What are you sorry about, Jim?'

'I needed sleep,' Brown said. 'I haven't slept for the past two days.' He began to eat again. 'This steak is good, huh?'

'You're quite a chef, Jim,' Perry said, 'and will you cut out calling me Buster? My name's Perry to you. Okay?'

'I'm with you. Sure.' Brown spoke with his mouth full of food. He ate savagely, the way a wolf eats. He paused to pour coffee and shoved a cup towards Perry. 'I can fix the phone, and the TV. I just wanted to be sure I could get some safe sleep. I didn't want you to start telephoning or to listen to the cop talk. I just had to have sleep.'

Perry began to lose his appetite. He began to push the food around on his plate.

'Are you in cop trouble, Jim?'

Brown wolfed down the last of the steak, then sat back. His thick lips moved into an ugly grin.

'Yeah.' He sipped coffee while he stared at Perry with his ice-cold eyes. 'That's for true. Cop trouble!' He brought his clenched fist down on the table in a thump. 'You can say that again.'

Perry found he couldn't finish his steak. He drank coffee while he looked anywhere but at Brown.

There was a long pause, while the rain continued to hammer against the windows, then Perry said quietly, 'Want to tell me about it?'

'Why not?' Brown finished his coffee and poured more. 'The big deal is if you want to hear about it.'

Perry pushed back his chair, stood up and crossed to the occasional table for a cigarette. He took time to light the cigarette, then returned to the table and sat down.

'Why the big deal?'

'Yeah.' Brown leaned forward, his powerful hands flat on the table. His ice-cold eyes stared at Perry. 'A good question.' With a flashing movement of his hand, Mason's .38 revolver appeared in his hand. The gun pointed directly at Perry. 'A good question.'

Perry felt a cold wave of fear run through him. He sat motionless.

'You don't have to do that, Jim,' he said, aware his voice was hoarse. 'If I can help you, I will.'

Brown studied him, grinned, and the gun went back into its holster.

'No, Perry, you won't *try* to help me. You are going to help me. Okay?'

'Can't you tell me what this is all about?' Perry said, relaxing.

'That's what I'm going to tell you. You like the coffee?'

'It's fine.'

'Yeah. I make good coffee. I cook well. There's not much else I can't do except make money.' The sour bitterness in Brown's voice bothered Perry. 'Now you, you write for the movies. Look at what you've got.' Brown waved in all directions around the room. 'Very fancy. You've got talent. I've got nothing.' He scowled. 'A guy like you wouldn't know what that means, to have nothing.'

Perry kept silent. He sat still, his heart thumping. He had a growing uneasiness that at any moment this man, sitting, staring at him, could turn violent.

'Nothing,' Brown repeated. 'You wouldn't know, would you, what nothing means?'

'That's where you're wrong,' Perry said. 'I'd guess you are not more than twenty-four. I am fourteen years older than you. When I was your age, I thought I had nothing. All I did was to sit around and read books. My parents kept pressing me to find some job, but all I wanted to do was sit and read. It wasn't until my parents were killed in a plane crash and I found there was no money that I was forced to get a job. I had to or I'd have starved. So I took up writing. I sat in a one-roomer and wrote and wrote. I lived on hamburgers if I was lucky. For two years I thought I was kidding myself. I kept thinking I had nothing. I didn't think anything of the book I was writing. There was a time when I was on a garbage-truck to earn eating money. I worked as a dishwasher in a greasy spoon, but I kept on writing. I finished the book. I still didn't think much of it, but a publisher did. It hit the best-seller's list. From then on, I wrote and wrote, and finally I got into the movie racket.' He paused to stub out his cigarette, then, looking directly at Brown, he went on, 'I do know what nothing means.'

He was surprised to see interest on the hard, unattractive face and surprised to see this man was listening.

'A garbage-truck, huh?' Brown said. 'That must have been rough.'

'It was eating money,' Perry said. 'At your age, it's a mistake to think you have nothing.'

'You know what I've got?' Brown leaned forward. 'If they catch me, I've got thirty years in the slammer.' He clenched his powerful hands into fists. 'Thirty years of nothing!'

Perry poured more coffee into his cup and pushed the pot towards Brown.

'What's the problem, Jim?' he asked. 'Look, we're here. We are stuck here as long as this rain lasts. Do you want to talk about it?'

Brown stared at him for a long moment, then got to his feet.

'Maybe.' He took up the dishes. 'I'll fix these. My old man was a cripple. My ma left him. I looked after him: did everything. I like doing things.' He carried the dishes into the kitchen and Perry heard him begin to wash up.

Perry finished his coffee, then carried the cup and saucer into the kitchen. Brown, at the sink, whistling tunelessly, ignored him. Perry put the cup and saucer down, then returned to the living-room. He sat down in one of the lounging chairs and listened to the rain.

Some situation! he thought. This had to be played very carefully. It was like having a tiger in the house. One false move and the tiger would strike. Perry was sure of this. He must relax. He must show no fear. Be casual, he told himself. Give this man no reason to turn vicious.

He forced himself to relax, stretching out his long legs and resting his head against the padded cushion of the chair. For a long ten minutes, he listened to the rain and the wind moaning in the trees, then Brown came in from the kitchen.

He watched Brown walk to the window, part the curtains and peer out. He stood with his broad back toward Perry for some minutes, then he pulled the curtains shut and moved to a lounging-chair near to the one in which Perry was sitting.

'You sure have more than nothing now,' he said as he sat down. 'That's a real fancy kitchen. You should have seen the hole I cooked my old man's meals in.'

'When I was your age, Jim, I didn't have a kitchen. I ate out of plastic sacks.'

'As long as this rain keeps up, they won't come looking for me,' Brown said, half to himself. 'Cops don't like getting wet.' He stared at Perry. 'You and me are going to keep company.' His thick lips moved into a sneering grin. 'Like the idea, Perry?'

'I'd rather have you here than be on my own in this goddamn rain,' Perry said mildly. 'At least, we won't starve. I was planning a fishing vacation. When I fish, I like to be on my own, but when I can't fish, I like company.' He was making a desperate effort to keep this man relaxed. 'You like fishing, Jim?' .

Brown looked at the wall clock, then got to his feet and went into the kitchen. He returned with Perry's transistor. He sat down.

'Time for the news,' he said and switched on the transistor.

The announcer was finishing the headlines. This country at war with that country. Vandals smashing shop windows. A black riot. Soldiers in Ireland getting shot. A bomb exploding in a Swiss bank. A Senator facing corruption charges.

Brown said, 'They're all crooks, Perry. We live in crap.'

'I guess,' Perry said. 'No one's happy.'

'Yeah, because most people like me have nothing.'

The announcer went on, *Before the weather forecast, we are again reading a police message. Chet Logan, the man who brutally murdered six people last night, is still at large. It is believed, wearing a Stetson hat and a slicker of a murdered patrol officer, he stopped a motorist and is heading South. Although this warning has been broadcast throughout the night, no motorist, so far, has notified the police. It is feared that the motorist could have been murdered and Logan is using the victim's car. You are asked to watch for this man. His description is as follows: age around twenty-four, powerfully built, blond. He has a cobra snake tattooed on his left arm. If you see a man resembling this description, telephone the Florida State police immediately. No attempt should be made to approach him. He is armed and very dangerous. Police road blocks have been set up between Jacksonville and Miami. The National Guard are co-operating with the State police. Every effort is being made to capture this man. This warning will be broadcast every hour.*

Brown snapped off the transistor and shoved it aside. He stared thoughtfully at the cobra snake tattooed on his arm, then he looked at Perry.

There was a long moment of silence. Perry felt cold. The words of the radio announcer were ringing in his mind. *Who brutally murdered six people last night . . . no attempt should be made to approach him . . . he is armed and very dangerous.*

Perry felt his mouth turn dry and his hands turn clammy, but he made a tremendous effort to appear casual.

'Chet Logan?' he said, wishing his voice didn't sound so husky. 'That you, Jim?'

Brown's thick lips twisted into a mirthless grin.

'Who else?' He again stared at the tattoo on his arm. 'You know something? Kids do stupid things . . . like this tattoo. This is just the kind of thing cops love. Stupid!' He rubbed the tattoo. 'When I was fifteen, I joined up with a gang. We called ourselves the Cobra. There were five of us. We had nothing . . . no money, no nothing. We went out nights and mugged suckers. That way I kept my old man in food, and paid the rent of our one room. Each of us had this snake tattooed on our left arm. Stupid! At the time, we thought it was terrific. Stupid!' He again rubbed the tattoo. 'Yeah, well, we were kids, and kids dig symbols. Stupid!' He looked up and stared past Perry. 'We were working over a rich mug when the cops arrived. I was the only one who got away.' Again his mirthless grin appeared. 'I'm good at getting away. The other four went into the slammer, but they didn't talk. It was a good gang while it lasted, so I got clear. When I returned home, I found my old man dead. I knew the finks in our block knew about my tattoo and would squeal to the cops, so I left my old man to rot and took off. I've been hoofing ever since . . . eight goddamn years, mugging, knocking off gas stations, living somehow, but the cops didn't catch up with me until last night.

I'm good at getting away, so I got away. No cop is ever going to catch me. Maybe, if I'm unlucky, he could kill me, but he'll never stick me behind bars.'

Perry had to know.

'Did you kill six people last night, Jim?'

'Oh sure.' Brown shrugged. 'What are six goddamn people in this crappy world when people are always killing each other? This six were stupid. They put pressure on me, and when anyone puts pressure on me I hit back. That's natural, isn't it?'

Perry felt in urgent need of a drink. He got up, went to the liquor-cabinet and poured himself a stiff shot of Scotch.

He heard Brown mutter something.

'I didn't get that, Jim. What did you say?'

Brown stared at him, his expression suddenly vicious.

'I said you can count yourself goddamn lucky you're not the seventh.'

Perry emptied his glass in one long gulp.

'How come I'm lucky?' he asked as he refilled his glass.

'I thought of knocking you off last night when you were drunk,' Brown said. 'Then I had a better idea. I listened to the radio. The National Guard! The cops! Sooner or later, they'll come here. They're going to check everywhere. So I got this better idea.' He paused, then went on, 'You're going to be my front. When the cops come, you'll tell them you're alone here. You'll cover for me.' He stabbed his short finger in Perry's direction. 'You give me away, and I promise you one thing.'

Perry waited, aware his heart was thumping. As Brown continued to glare at him, he asked, 'What do you promise me?'

The unattractive, square-shaped face turned into a snarling mask.

'We'll share a double funeral,' Brown said. 'That's what I promise.'

'The footpath is just ahead,' Ross said, peering through the windshield. 'Pull into this lay-by.'

Hollis slowed, then steered the car into the lay-by and cut the engine.

'From here, we walk,' Ross said. He fiddled with the radio and got Jenner's headquarters. 'Carl, Ross,' he said. 'We are at P on the Miami highway. We're using the footpath to get down to the river.'

'Hold it!' Jenner said, his voice sharp. 'You wait. Jacklin has sent four Guards and they'll be with you in half an hour. I don't want you to go into the forest without support, Jeff.'

'I have all the support I need,' Ross said. 'I have Hank. I don't want four trigger-happy kids losing themselves in this jungle. Keep them off my back. Over and out,' and he switched off. 'Okay, Hank, let's get wet.'

The two men reached into the overhead rack for their rifles. Ross put the plastic sack of sandwiches in the pocket of his slicker, then both men got out into the rain.

After locking the car, Hank followed Ross's broad back along a narrow path that led into the forest. Once under the heavy foliage of the trees, they were sheltered from the pelting rain, but water dripped on them. Water and mud flooded the path, making the going slow and precarious.

This walk reminded Hollis of his trips into the Vietnamese jungles. Often it rained like this, but, as he had led his patrol, he hadn't bothered about the rain. All he then bothered about was a concealed sniper. He felt pretty confident that this killer wouldn't be lurking in the shrubs. All the same, he kept his rifle at the ready as he plodded after Ross.

Here was a man! Hollis thought. One of the real old toughies. A man to be admired.

This is my territory, he had said to the top shot of the Florida police, no one gives me orders.

That's telling them, Hollis thought, and grinned.

Ross paused and turned.

'Another mile, Hank, then we reach the river. The first fishing-lodge is immediately at the end of the footpath. I'll go forward, you cover me. We don't stop to argue.

We shoot first and apologise after. Okay?'

'Look, Sheriff,' Hollis said quietly. 'I've had jungle training in the army. With respect, I go first and you cover me. This is my scene. We don't want to make a balls-up of this. One slip and we're both dead. Okay?'

Ross hesitated for only a moment, then he nodded.

'Right. Then let's get on with it. Go straight ahead. I'll do what you do.'

Hollis moved around Ross and started down the path. The trees were thinning so both men had the rain beating down on them.

After half an hour of slow progress, sloshing in the mud and rain, Ross said softly, 'We're nearly there, Hank.'

Pushing aside a tree branch, Hollis could see the river. He could also see a wooden cabin.

'That's Mr Greenstein's place. He only comes once a year,' Ross said. He fumbled in his pocket and produced a bunch of keys. 'They all leave their keys with me.' While the rain dripped off his Stetson hat, he selected a key. 'What do you think?'

'You stay here, Sheriff. I'll take a look,' Hollis said, and taking the key from Ross, he moved fast in a crouch towards the cabin.

Watching him, Ross saw his deputy really knew his business. He seemed to melt into the trees and shrubs, moving like a shadow with the speed of a hunting panther.

Ross stayed where he was, fingering his rifle. He felt bad about letting Hollis do this, but he knew the younger man could handle this dangerous situation much better than he could. He thought of Tom Mason who had driven up to Loss's farm and to his death. He should never have let him go up there alone. Now, he had let his second deputy go forward alone. Suppose Hank got killed? Trying to imitate Hollis's movements, Ross moved forward until he was within twenty yards of the cabin. Crouching, he covered the cabin with his rifle, listened and waited.

He waited for perhaps ten minutes. They were the longest minutes he could remember, then he saw Hollis appear around the side of the cabin and wave to him.

Relieved, Ross hurried to him.

'Can't see a trace of a break-in, Sheriff,' Hollis said. 'All the window shutters are tight. The door's okay, but he could be in there.'

'We'll check it out.'

It was a nervy half hour before Ross relocked the door of the deserted cabin.

Both men now fully realised the task they faced. As they had checked the four rooms of the cabin they had known that any moment there could be a blast of gun fire. It had been a nerve-stretching job: four more cabins to check!

'The next one belongs to Mr Franklin. He comes here regularly twice a year. He's due at the end of the month.'

'Who looks after these cabins while they're empty?' Hollis asked.

'My wife, Mary, organises it. These guys let her know when they are coming and she sends a couple of women down to clean up. Franklin's place is about two hundred yards further on.'

Again Hollis led the way. Again there was tension. Again Hollis checked for a break-in. Again the two men searched the cabin. Both men were very edgy by now. By the time they had checked out the fourth cabin, the time was 15.45.

Standing in the big lounge, Ross took off his soaking slicker.

'I guess we'll take a break, Hank. Let's eat. There's only one more cabin to check. If he isn't there, then I guess he isn't in the forest. There's nowhere else for him to hide.'

Hollis took off his slicker, wiped his face with a handkerchief and sat down.

Ross produced the ham sandwiches and the two men ate hungrily.

'The last cabin we have to check, Hank,' Ross said as he munched, 'belongs to Mr Perry Weston, who is a movie script-writer. He's a real nice fellow: lots of money, has a place on Long Island. He bought this lodge around three years ago, and had it worked over: made it real fancy. For the first year, he came every other month. He's a keen fisherman. Many a time I had drinks with him at his lodge or in Rockville. Then he married a girl fourteen years or so younger than he. Fishing wasn't her scene. Mr Weston wrote to Mary asking her to look after the place, saying one day, he hoped to be back. Mary goes to the lodge every month and keeps it nice. He hasn't shown up these past two years, but Mary keeps a check on the freezer. There's plenty of food. The lodge would be a gift to Logan.'

Hollis finished his sandwich, then looked at his watch. The time was 16.05.

'It'll be getting dark in a couple of hours. Shall we go?'

'Yeah.' Ross stood up and stretched. He put on his slicker. 'Looks like the rain's lessening.'

The two men picked up their rifles and left the cabin. Hollis waited until Ross had locked up, then started down the muddy path by the river.

'About a half mile ahead,' Ross said.

Moving silently, still hampered by the mud and water that covered the path, the two men began to converge on Perry Weston's fishing-lodge.

Jim Brown had repaired the plug on the TV set, had turned the set on and, for the past hour, sat watching a police movie. From time to time, he released a derisive whistle.

'Cops don't act this way,' he muttered. 'What crap!'

Perry sat away from the set, nursing a glass of Scotch. The loud voices, the sound of gun fire, the roaring cars didn't disturb his worried thoughts.

When people put pressure on me, I hit back. That's natural, isn't it? I promise you. You give me away and we'll share a double funeral.

Perry recalled the vicious expression on Brown's face when he had said this. He was sure Brown wouldn't hesitate to wipe him out if Perry made one false move.

Jesus! he thought. What a situation! He had to do everything he could think of to keep this man relaxed: no pressure: no criticism: friendly understanding. Listen to him, Perry said to himself. Go along with him. Let him talk when he wants to.

The movie came to an end and Brown switched off the set.

'Junk,' he said. 'Do you write junk like that, Perry?'

'I hope not. I don't write for TV.'

'No,' Brown turned in his chair and stared at Perry. 'I guess you're pretty smart. You make a lot of money?'

Keep this ape relaxed, Perry told himself as he said, 'I make more than I did when I was your age.'

'How much money do you make?'

'It depends. Each year varies. Around sixty thousand, but it's taxed.' Perry made much more than this, but he wasn't going to tell this man just how much he did earn.

'Sixty thousand . . . nice. Have you got money here?'

'Around five hundred.'

'You could get more?'

'Yes, from the Rockville bank.'

'That's good news. I will need a stake, Perry. Okay with you?'

Perry forced a smile.

'Okay with me, Jim.'

Brown nodded again.

'It'll have to be okay with you, Perry, right down the line.'

'Looks like it.'

'Yeah. Sixty thousand bucks. Know the biggest sum of money I lifted off a sucker? Two hundred dollars and a gold watch that wasn't gold.'

'People don't carry much money around with them these days.'

'That's right, but you can get money from the bank?'

Perry nodded.

Brown got to his feet and went to the window. Lifting aside the curtain, he peered out.

'The rain's stopping. That means the cops could be here before long.' He turned and stared at Perry, his ice-cold eyes menacing. 'You know what to say when they come?'

'You've already spelt it out,' Perry said quietly. 'We don't have to go over the dialogue again.'

'Just don't play it tricky. That way, you stay alive. Understand?'

'I hear you. So I don't play it tricky.'

Brown's thick lips parted in a grin.

'You're smart. Any guy who works on a garbage-truck and ends up with a joint like this must be smart, so don't play it tricky.'

'So, okay, I'm smart,' Perry said. 'One thing, Jim, if the police do come here, you've left the Stetson hat and the slicker in my garage. If they find them . . .' He stopped as he saw Brown's sneering grin.

'Listen, smart guy, I don't get caught. I've got the hat and the slicker hidden in my room,' Brown said. 'You don't have to worry about me. All you have to do is worry about yourself.'

Perry shrugged.

'I have things in the car. Clothes, a typewriter, business papers. I'd like to have them. Okay with you?'

Brown thought for a long moment, then he nodded. He took from his pocket the key to the garage door.

'Go ahead. Unload the car. Nothing tricky. Let me tell you something. I'm good at two things. I cooked for my old man who liked his food. That's one thing I'm good at.' The gun in its holster flashed into his hand. 'I'm very good with a gun. Go ahead, get your stuff, but no tricks . . . right?'

Hollis lifted his hand as a signal to Ross, plodding through the mud and rain, to stop. Under the dripping trees, the two men came together.

'Someone's in Weston's lodge,' Hollis whispered. 'A man's just come out of the garage. There's a car there.'

They were within fifteen yards of the fishing-lodge. Ross moved forward and peered through the rain. He recognised Perry Weston as he was unloading baggage from a car.

With Hollis crouching by his side, he said, 'That's Mr Weston.'

'You mean that's the owner of the place?'

'That's him.'

For a long moment, they watched Perry drag out two suitcases, then he disappeared from sight.

Ross moved out of the cover of the trees with Hollis at his heels.

Brown, watching, spotted the Stetson hats.

Perry came into the living-room and dumped the suitcases.

'I've got my typewriter to collect,' he said.

'Take it easy, buster,' Brown said softly. 'They're here. Two goddamn cops. You know what to do. One stupid move from you and you're dead. Go ahead and get your typewriter.'

Perry gaped at him.

'They're here? What do you mean?'

'Get moving or there'll be a shoot-out, and the first to go will be you! Go!'

The threat in Brown's voice was like a blast of icy wind to Perry. For a long moment he stood paralysed. Brown gave him a shove, then ran up the stairs.

'I'll be watching, buster,' he called. 'One stupid move and you're dead.'

Bracing himself, Perry walked back to the garage.

5

Ted Fleichman sat in his car, parked opposite the Westons'
house, feeling like a lump of jelly. Sweat ran down his
face. His hands, resting on the steering-wheel, trembled.

Jesus! he was thinking. That vicious little bitch! He
recalled the sound of the bullet as it had zipped past his
face. An inch to the right and he would have been dead!
What a mug he had been to have under-estimated this girl!
Man! This could cause real trouble! Suppose she called the
cops? He wiped more sweat off his face and made an effort
to control his shattered nerves.

No, he assured himself, she wouldn't call the cops. She
was too smart to do that. She'd not only land him in
trouble, but herself.

He had had enough of Sheila Weston. He wanted out.
He would tell Dorrie to take him off the assignment. Let
Fred handle this bitch, and good luck to him!

Sunday the office was closed. So, okay. He wasn't going
to sit in the car outside her house, taking a chance the cops
could descend on him. He thought of his sick wife. He
couldn't remember when last they had spent Sunday
together. He was always watching some randy woman or
randy man seven days of the week.

Well, okay, he would go home. His wife would be surprised and pleased. He'd take her out for dinner this evening. To hell with the cost! To hell with Sheila Weston! He
started the car's engine and pulled away from the kerb. He
could always tell the office that he had a stomach upset.
To hell with them anyway! Now, relaxing, he drove
homewards.

Sheila stood at the window and watched him go. She had quickly come out of her faint and had walked unsteadily into the living-room. She had stood behind the muslin curtains, watching Fleichman as he sat in his car. Then when she saw him pull away from the kerb, she drew in a long breath of relief. He was going!

She moved away from the window and sat down in one of the lounging-chairs. For some twenty minutes, she stared into space, her mind active. What an experience! she thought. This must never happen again. Then her mind shifted to her husband.

What's the matter with me? she asked herself. Why do I act like a goddamn tramp?

Perry!

She felt an overwhelming need to be with him. Ever since they had married, he had been kind and understanding. Whenever he hadn't been writing, he had been more than lovable. He had always spoilt her. Although she had been demanding, he had done his best to please her.

She beat her clenched fists on her knees.

The trouble with you, you stupid bitch, she thought, is you're over-sexed. You have only to look at any handsome man and you want him to stick it in you. This must stop! Perry is marvellous in bed. He loves you! These other men just want your body, but Perry really loves you! I want him and I need him!

She thought back on her various lovers, then she thought of Julian Lucan. She moaned to herself. What a mad, reckless fool she had been!

This must stop!

Then she remembered what Fleichman had said when she had asked him who was employing him to watch her.

Nothing to do with Mr Weston. I can't name my client. That would be a breach of confidence.

Her expression hardened. Ever since Perry had become the top script-writer, she had felt that he was dominated by Silas S. Hart. She had once met this man and had hated him. She knew he had no time for her. When any man didn't fall for her, she automatically hated him. She had an instinctive feeling this powerful movie mogul would like nothing better than to break up their marriage.

So it was obvious: this ghastly blackmailer's client was Silas S. Hart!

She remembered Mavis had said Perry had been seen by her husband at Jacksonville airport, yet Perry had told her he was going to Los Angeles to work for Hart, so why should he be in Florida?

She sat back, thinking. This was another of Hart's dirty tricks to separate them. This fishing-lodge Perry had so often talked to her about, had tried so hard to persuade her to go there with him!

Yes, he must be there.

She had a suffocating urge to get away from this house, to be with Perry, to talk to him. She had to confess. Perry was always understanding.

Jumping to her feet, she ran up to the bedroom. As she began to pack a suitcase, she felt released. In a few hours, she would be with Perry. She would tell him everything. She would ask that they might begin afresh. Why not? They *could* begin afresh.

Anything, she thought as she closed the suitcase, rather than stay alone in this house.

Packed, dressed, she carried the suitcase down to the lobby and called the airport. She was told a flight to Jacksonville was due off in two hours. Sheila booked a reservation. She had plenty of time.

Again she went to the window. There was no car parked outside the house. She felt a moment of triumph. She had frightened this filthy blackmailer away. So, for the moment, she was no longer being watched!

She scribbled a hasty note to Liz, telling her she would be away for a week or so, and to look after the house. Then she telephoned for a taxi. She then went into the lobby to wait for the taxi and she saw the gun lying on the floor by the front door where she had dropped it when she had fainted.

As she saw the gun, the shock of realising that she had

nearly committed murder made her close her eyes. God! she thought. What a mess I'm in!

Perry! He would be the solution! She must tell him everything!

She picked up the gun and stuffed it into her handbag, not knowing what else to do with it.

Seventy minutes later, she was at the airport. Half an hour later, sitting relaxed in the aircraft, she was heading for Jacksonville.

Sheriff Ross and Deputy Sheriff Hollis standing just behind him, watched Perry return to the garage.

'I'll go talk to him,' Ross said. 'You keep out of sight. Let's take it easy, huh?'

'I'll cover you, Sheriff,' Hollis said. 'You take it easy. Logan could be there.'

Ross walked slowly towards the lighted garage, his rifle at the alert. He arrived at the entrance of the garage as Perry heaved the typewriter from the car's boot.

'Hi, there, Mr Weston,' Ross said.

Perry was braced for this encounter, although he didn't expect to see Sheriff Ross. He put down the typewriter and forced a smile.

'Why, hello, Jeff!' He came forward. 'What are you doing here in this weather?'

The two men shook hands.

'I could say the same to you, Mr Weston,' Ross said. 'You couldn't have come at a worse time.'

'I guess you're right. I'm working on a movie, and thought I'd get away from the big city. I didn't expect to run into this.'

'You just arrived, Mr Weston?'

'Got in late last night. The road down here is murder. I guess I was lucky to make it.'

'You on your own, Mr Weston?'

'That's right.'

'All okay with the lodge?'

'Sure.' Perry made the effort and, forcing a smile, he went on, 'A million thanks to Mary. The place is fine.'

Ross turned and signalled to Hollis who came forward. 'This, Mr Weston, is my new deputy: Hank Hollis.'

'Glad to know you, Hollis,' Perry said as the two men shook hands. 'Rifles, huh? You two can't be out hunting?'

'That's what we're doing,' Ross said quietly.

'Well, what do you know?' Perry was trying desperately to sound casual. 'Come on in. You'd like coffee or something?'

'We won't come in,' Ross said. 'We'd only muddy up your place.' He pointed to his mud-encrusted boots.

'Come on! Take them off! I bet you could use some coffee. You two look half drowned.'

Ross and Hollis exchanged glances, then Ross nodded. 'Thanks, Mr Weston. We sure could use some coffee.'

'Get those boots off and come on in. I'll start coffee,' Perry said, picking up the typewriter. 'You know the way, don't you?'

As both men stripped off their slickers and their boots, Ross said quietly, 'Keep alert, Hank. I guess it's okay, but don't let's take chances.'

'The rifles?' Hollis asked.

'Leave them here.' Ross patted his revolver holster. 'Just let's watch it, Hank.'

He led the way into the big living-room, both men in their stocking feet.

In the kitchen, Perry poured coffee into a saucepan. He had no idea where Brown was hiding. Upstairs? He could be anywhere. *We'll share a double funeral.* He was surprised to find how steady his nerves had become. He no longer felt frightened. This situation was developing into a plot for a movie script: the kind of script Silas S. Hart was wanting. He paused for a moment, thinking. He realised he was playing with fire. Any moment Brown could turn vicious, but it was possible, if he played the cards carefully, Brown could be kept under control.

Perry felt a surge of confidence. He knew for certain that if he gave Ross the slightest hint that Brown was hiding somewhere in the lodge, there would be a shoot-out. He knew for sure Brown would never be taken alive.

Some situation! Already, he could imagine how to begin the script. He poured coffee into two mugs. So, okay, play this very cool. This could develop into a great movie.

He carried the two mugs into the living-room to find the two officers standing awkwardly, looking around.

'Make yourselves at home,' he said. 'Sit down. Here . . .' He handed the two mugs of coffee to the two men, then dropped into a lounging-chair. 'You didn't tell me. What are you two doing out here in this goddamn rain?'

Both men sat down, facing him.

'Well, Mr Weston, we're hunting a killer,' Ross said. 'I had an idea he might be hiding in one of the fishing-lodges. We've checked them out. So, I was wrong.'

'A killer? You don't mean this man Logan? I picked up a radio warning.'

'That's the man.' Ross paused, then went on, 'Would you remember Jud Loss, Mr Weston?'

Perry had a sudden cold feeling in the pit of his stomach.

'Jud Loss? Why, sure. He owns an orange-farm. We used to have a drink when he was in the village. Nice fellow. What about him?'

'Ever met his wife? His daughter?'

'Can't say I met his wife, but I remember his daughter . . . nice kid. What about him?'

'Logan arrived at the farm and massacred the three of them with an axe.'

'Good God!' Perry stared at Ross in horror. 'They're dead?'

'My deputy, Tom Mason, went out to the farm. He was unlucky. Logan gave him the same axe treatment.' Ross jerked his thumb at Hollis. 'He's replaced Mason.'

Into Perry's mind flashed the hesitant thought. Should he tell these men that Brown was here?

We'll share a double funeral.

No!

'This is a terrible thing, Jeff,' he said. 'Do you think this man is still in the district?'

'He could be. The State police and the National Guard are hunting for him. The State police think he held up a motorist and got through the roadblocks and is in Miami.'

Perry nodded. He was sure, somewhere, Brown was listening, gun in hand.

Having finished his coffee, Ross got to his feet.

'We've got to get along, Mr Weston. Will you be staying long?'

'A couple of weeks.' Perry heaved himself out of his chair. 'Could be longer. It depends how the work goes.'

'Do you want my wife to look after you, Mr Weston?'

'Not right now, Jeff. I'll telephone her . . . okay?'

'You do that. I guess the rain will clear by tomorrow. It's been a rough three days.'

'Let's hope.' Perry went with them to the garage and waited until the two men had put on their boots and struggled into their soaked slickers. He shook hands.

'I'll be around, Jeff, but for the next week, I've a big job to cope with. Give Mary my love. I'll call her when I need help.'

'Okay, Mr Weston.' Ross said, picking up his rifle. 'Best of luck for the movie.'

He and Hollis moved out into the rain and started up the muddy path into the forest.

'Well, I guess I was wrong,' Ross said. 'Okay, you can't always be right. I guess Jacklin makes sense when he thinks Logan got through to Miami where he could get lost.'

Hollis said nothing. He plodded through the mud behind Ross, but when they reached the shelter of the dripping forest he said, 'Hold it a moment, Sheriff.'

Ross stopped and turned.

'What is it, Hank?'

'I think Logan could be in Weston's place, and Weston, under gun threat, is covering for him.'

'What are you saying?' Ross stared at Hollis. 'How can you say a thing like that?'

'A hunch, Sheriff,' Hollis said quietly. 'I've got a hunch that Logan is there.'

'A hunch? What do you mean?'

'Maybe you can tell me something, Sheriff.' Hollis's

voice was cold and hard. 'Why is the telephone connection torn out of the wall? While you were talking to Weston, I was looking around. Do you think Weston would yank out the telephone cable, killing the telephone?'

Ross stiffened. He felt suddenly old. He should have seen what Hollis had seen.

'We'll go back. We'll ask Mr Weston . . .'

'With respect, Sheriff,' Hollis said, 'we shouldn't do that. You don't want Mr Weston killed, do you?'

Having plodded miles in mud and rain, Ross felt tired and defeated. He made the effort to say, 'You really think Logan is holed up there?'

'I don't know. He could be. Why the disconnected telephone?'

Ross thought.

'You think if Logan's holed up here, he'll start shooting?'

'What's he got to lose? If we move in, the first to go will be Weston.'

'You could be wrong, couldn't you? Mr Weston said he was alone.'

'You'd say that if you knew a gun was pointing at you.'

With his boots in thick mud and feeling the rain dripping on his Stetson hat, Ross felt baffled. Up to now, Rockville had been free of crime. Now he realised that he had a situation that, tired and feeling old, he couldn't handle.

'We'd better alert the State police,' he said.

'With respect, Sheriff,' Hollis said quietly, 'that wouldn't be the way to play it. Frontal assault, if Logan is there, wouldn't save Weston's life. He'd be the first to go.'

Ross thought, then nodded.

'So how do you suggest we handle it, Hank?'

'We should let this situation cool. If Logan is there, holding a gun on Weston, and I could be wrong, but if he is, I want him to think we don't think he is there. That way he could relax, and when a killer like him relaxes, then we can make our move.'

'What move, Hank?'

'With your permission, Sheriff, I want to come back

here tomorrow. When I was in the army, I trained as an anti-sniper. I know how to watch and wait. I want your permission, Sheriff, to do just that: watch and wait. If Logan is there and he feels there's no pressure on him, he could relax, and that's the time to nail him. Suppose we go back to the office and talk about it?'

'I don't like it, Hank,' Ross said, hesitating. 'If Logan is there, Mr Weston is in danger. I think we should go back and search the lodge.'

'If we do that, and Logan is there, Weston's a dead man. We too could be dead. Do me a favour? Play it my way. Let it cool; let me watch.'

Ross turned this over in his mind. He felt confident that Hollis was talking sense, but still he hesitated, remembering Tom Mason.

'When I was serving in Vietnam,' Hollis said quietly, 'a sniper knocked off twenty young men. It took me ten days, hidden in the jungle, to get him. Finally the bastard relaxed and I spotted him. Sheriff, this is a specialist's job. I'm a specialist. Watch and wait. Will you let me play it my way?'

Ross put his hand on Hollis's shoulder.

'Okay, son,' he said. 'We'll do it your way, but I must report to Jenner.'

Hollis shook his head.

'Again with respect, Sheriff, we should tell no one. I'll come back here tomorrow evening, and I'll watch. We'll keep in touch by radio. If you tell Jenner, he'll start action, and that's what we don't want right now. We don't know if Logan is there, so don't tell anyone.'

Ross shrugged helplessly.

'Okay.'

He turned and began to plod along the path, then he paused.

'I'll have to tell Jenner something'

'Sure.' Hollis grinned. 'I suggest you tell him we've checked out the fishing-lodges, and we haven't found Logan. We haven't found him yet, have we, Sheriff?'

*　*　*

Would you remember Jud Loss, his wife and daughter?
Logan arrived at the farm and massacred the three of them
with an axe.

Perry leaned against the Toyota, feeling sick. He vividly
remembered Jud Loss: a short, thickset man with ginger-
coloured hair. Loss often came down to the Rockville bar,
and he and Perry often had beers together.

Murdered!

He would make a break for it! Run after Ross! Get away
from this nightmare.

'Very nice, Perry.' Brown's hard clipped voice made his
heart skip a beat. He turned.

Brown was standing in the doorway, gun in hand.

'Very nice,' Brown repeated. 'Come on in, Perry. We
both can relax, huh? Those slobs won't be coming back.
You played it really cool.' The gun waved at Perry. 'Come
on in.'

Under the threat of the gun, Perry walked unsteadily
into the living-room. He heard Brown lock the garage
door, then he came into the room.

'For handling that, Perry,' Brown said, 'I'll cook you a
nice supper. Like a chicken?'

Perry sat down.

'I don't want anything.'

'Sure you do. You want a big Scotch.' Brown dropped
the gun into its holster and crossed to the liquor cabinet.
He poured Scotch, came back to Perry and thrust the glass
into his hand. 'You'll be okay in a moment. My old man
was a lush. When I could steal a bottle, Scotch always
cheered him up.'

Perry swallowed the drink in one long, greedy gulp,
then he shuddered and dropped the glass onto the floor.

Brown sat on the arm of a lounging-chair, watching.

'You filthy brute!' Perry blurted out. 'You killed a good
friend of mine!'

Brown shrugged.

'I didn't know. If I had known it wouldn't have made
any difference. The stupid jerk put me under pressure. I
get mad when jerks put me under pressure. Here's what
happened. There was this car crash and the two cops got

killed. I took off. I walked and ran in the rain for ten miles. I hadn't eaten for two days. I was bloody hungry. I came to this farm. I banged on the door. This jerk opened up. I asked him for food.' Brown's face hardened. 'Know what he said to me? He said "Get the hell off my land. I don't give hand-outs to bums!" and he slammed the door. I had nowhere to go. I was wetter than a drowned dog. Know something, Perry? When I want something and some stupid jerk won't part, I get mad and, when I get mad, it's just too bad for stupid jerks. I found the axe in a shed. I went back and kicked the door in. I found the jerk and his wife settling to a hot meal. I fixed them. Then I heard a scream and there was a girl coming down the stairs. Her screams got me madder so I chased her up to her room and fixed her. Then I went downstairs and ate the meal on the table. It was good.' Brown nodded. 'Yeah, it sure was good. The telephone bell kept ringing. I guessed it was the cops, checking. I guessed before long, they'd come up to check, so I hid in the shed. When I saw there was only one of them, I fixed him and took his car. That's how it happened, Perry. All stupid jerks.' He stared for a long, hard moment at Perry. 'Don't you be a stupid jerk. Now, I'll go fix a chicken dinner. Give yourself another drink.' He got to his feet, then paused. Watching him, Perry saw Brown's face turn into a snarling, vicious mask. The sight of his murderous-looking face sent a chill down Perry's spine.

He saw Brown was staring at the disconnected telephone cable.

'Goddamn it!' Brown muttered. 'I should have fixed that.' He turned. 'They didn't say anything, did they? I was listening. Maybe they didn't spot it. The old fart is harmless, but the other guy looked tough.' His eyes narrowed. 'I'll take a look. You sit right here. Don't be a stupid jerk.'

Perry heard him run upstairs. A moment later, he came back, wearing Tom Mason's slicker.

'I'll take a look,' he said and, opening the front door, he disappeared into the growing gloom and rain.

Perry got to his feet and poured himself another Scotch.

93

There was nothing he could do, he told himself. The Scotch had got him over the shock of hearing the Loss family had been murdered. He returned to his chair, lit a cigarette and sipped the drink. He looked at his watch. The time was now 19.10. Already it was turning dark. He thought of the night ahead. How long would this man remain here? He finished his drink. He now felt relaxed and a little high.

Would Ross and Hollis return? Had they spotted the telephone cable? Did they suspect Brown was here?

He got to his feet and began to prowl around the room. Brown would never be taken alive. *We'll share a double funeral*. For the first time in his life, Perry realised how important life was to him. He had to do everything he could to prevent a shoot out, knowing that he would be the first to get shot.

It was over half an hour before Brown appeared silently in the living-room. After his third Scotch, Perry was dozing in the armchair. He came awake with a start as Brown closed the door.

'They've gone,' Brown said. 'Stupid jerks! They couldn't have spotted the telephone. Cops! They don't know their asses from their elbows! I followed them right to their car. They've gone!'

Perry heaved a sigh of relief.

'Okay, Perry, I'll fix supper,' Brown said. 'You hungry now?'

Perry discovered he was hungry.

'Sure.'

'Tonight,' Brown said, 'you get locked in your room. I sleep light, Perry. If there's trouble, I'll handle it. Understand?'

'Sure,' Perry said.

Nodding, Brown went into the kitchen. Perry heard him whistling tunelessly as he put the chicken on the spit.

Sheila Weston wheeled the hand trolley containing her suitcase and vanity-box into the arrival centre of Jacksonville's airport.

It had to be raining! she thought. She had no idea where to find Perry's fishing-lodge. All she knew was it was near some village called Rockville.

Describing the lodge, Perry had told her it was right by the river. He had said hopefully he would teach her to fish. Sheila had firmly declined.

'I don't like walking, I've seen a river and to hell with fishing,' she had said.

That settled that.

Now aching to talk to Perry, she was determined to get to the fishing-lodge. The Hertz Rental people would probably know. Perry had said he always rented a car to get to the lodge.

The time now was 19.15, and she could see through the glass doors not only steady rain, but the light was failing.

As Sheila approached the Hertz desk, she saw a broad-shouldered man, his back to her, leaning on the counter, talking to a pretty Hertz clerk who was smiling the way young girls smile when a man has made his mark.

Sheila eyed the man's broad back. He was wearing a beautifully cut, lavender-coloured country suit. His dark hair was shot with grey.

She left the trolley and walked up to the desk.

The Hertz girl was saying, 'I really wouldn't advise it, Mr Franklin. Better wait until tomorrow.' She then looked at Sheila and said, 'I won't be a minute.'

The man turned and regarded Sheila.

She felt a little jolt run through her. This was some man! She immediately thought of Douglas Fairbanks Jr when he was in his prime. This man had the same kind of features, not only that, but he had a personality that came out of him, and made Sheila feel randy.

'Attend to the lady, Penny,' the man said. 'I'm in no rush.'

The girl lost her enchanted smile and moved along the counter.

'What can I do for you, madam?'

'I am Mrs Perry Weston,' Sheila said. 'Did my husband hire a car from you yesterday?'

The girl's face lit up. Even remembering the thrill of dealing with Perry Weston remained.

'Why, yes, madam.'

'How do I get to Rockville and his fishing-lodge? Would you know?'

The girl looked blank.

'Rockville, yes, but Mr Weston's fishing-lodge, no.'

The man whom the Hertz girl had called Mr Franklin said in a deep, soft voice that sent a tingle down Sheila's spine, 'Excuse me. I couldn't help but overhear. I am Perry's neighbour. I have a fishing-lodge about a mile from his.'

Sheila turned her back on the Hertz girl and gave Franklin a flashing smile.

'What a coincidence, Mr Franklin. I believe Perry has mentioned your name.' This was strictly untrue.

'I'm going to Rockville and could show you the way, but not tonight. Miss Pentagast tells me the roads down there are bad. Perhaps your husband is meeting you?'

Sheila flashed a smile as she moved away from the desk, aware the Hertz girl was listening. Franklin moved after her until they were away from the desk.

'It's a surprise visit,' Sheila said. 'No, he doesn't know I'm coming.'

Franklin lifted an eyebrow.

'You won't make it tonight, Mrs Weston, but tomorrow, if the rain clears, I'll be happy to drive you there.'

'That's very kind of you, Mr Franklin. Well, I guess I'll have to find a hotel.' Sheila put on her helpless look which had paid dividends in the past. 'Do you know of a good hotel, Mr Franklin?'

Franklin studied her for a brief, searching moment, then he smiled.

'I come down here every other month,' he said. 'Sure, there'a an excellent motel I stay at. Would you like me to make arrangements for you, Mrs Weston?'

Again the helpless look.

'I don't want to be a nuisance . . .'

'It'd be my pleasure. I'll get a taxi. Just leave your baggage. Maybe you will want to telephone your husband?'

Oh, no, Sheila thought. What she felt was the urgent need to get into bed with this beautiful man.

'I don't think so. He would only fuss. I'll call him tomorrow.'

They regarded each other, both smiling.

'I'll fix everything for you, Mrs Weston. Just wait here.'

Sheila sat down on one of the benches while Franklin wheeled her trolley outside.

You never know, she thought, what's around the corner, then she remembered Julian Lucan. Who was this man, Franklin? He must be all right if he had a fishing-lodge and knew Perry. All the same, Lucan haunted her. He too had been suave, handsome and sexy. She got to her feet and walked to the Hertz desk. The Hertz girl looked inquiringly at her.

'Who is Mr Franklin?' Sheila asked. 'What does he do?'

The girl gave a sly little smile. She read the message.

'Mr Franklin is the senior partner of Franklin & Bernstein, the New York lawyers, Mrs Weston.' Her sly smile widened. 'You could say he was important people.'

The two girls exchanged looks, then Sheila smiled.

'Thank you,' she said, and returned to her seat.

Well, that's all right, she thought. Maybe he won't want me in his bed. Maybe . . .

After five or six minutes, Franklin appeared.

'Sorry for the delay. I had trouble getting rooms at the motel. Everyone seems to be staying over-night, but I've fixed it. Are you ready to go?'

'It is kind of you, Mr Franklin,' Sheila said in her most demure manner.

'Since we could be near neighbours, suppose you call me Gene?'

'Of course. Sheila.'

'Nice name.' Franklin took her elbow and steered her out to a waiting taxi.

On the brief drive to the motel, he said, 'Would you dine with me, Sheila?'

'I'd love to.'

When they reached the imposing-looking motel, Sheila could see just how important Gene Franklin was. The staff bowed and scraped. The luggage was whisked away. Franklin shook hands with a beaming reception clerk. Two bellboys conducted them down a corridor and opened two doors.

'That's yours, Sheila,' Franklin said, generously tipping. 'Suppose we meet in the foyer at eight thirty?'

'Of course.'

Leaving him, she entered the big, comfortably furnished bedroom. Her luggage was already on the rack. She shut the door and looked around, then her smile brightened. There was a communicating door to Franklin's room.

She spent half an hour lying in a warm bath, relaxing. For this night, Perry was forgotten, also Julian Lucan and that ghastly blackmailer Fleichman. Sheila was happy.

Forty minutes later, she was being guided into the crowded restaurant by Gene Franklin, who gently held her elbow. The touch of his warm hand sent thrills through Sheila's body.

The Maître d' was there. Chairs were pulled out. Menus flourished.

'An aperitif, perhaps, Mr Franklin?'

'A martini, Sheila?'

'That would be lovely.'

'Two,' Franklin said. As the Maître d' whisked away, he went on, 'Do you like sea food, Sheila?'

'I adore it.'

'Then let me suggest. They do shrimps steamed in beer. Sounds odd, but it is excellent. Then I suggest a small steak and half a lobster with crabmeat stuffing.'

'Sounds utterly marvellous.'

Two martinis appeared on the table. The Maître d' arrived and took the order.

'Perhaps honey biscuits or a tossed salad?'

'No honey biscuits. Salad please,' Sheila said.

'Me too,' Franklin said. 'Their honey biscuits are excellent. Sure?'

'Oh no. I have to watch my weight.'

The Maître d' went away.

'Watch your weight?' Franklin looked directly at her, his handsome face smiling. 'I should have thought you had other things to watch.'

Sheila stiffened.

'Oh? What makes you say that? What other things.'

His smile widened.

'You would know better than I would, wouldn't you, Sheila?'

She suddenly felt a little uneasy.

'I really don't know what you are talking about.'

'Never mind.' He produced a solid-gold cigarette case. 'Smoke?'

'Not now, thank you.' She sipped her drink, regarding him. He was certainly one of the most handsome men she had ever met. *I should have thought you had other things to watch.* What an odd thing to have said. She shrugged off the remark.

'I don't know how long you will be staying at your husband's lodge,' Franklin said, 'but you'll need all-weather clothes. Did you bring things with you?'

'All weather?'

'There are floods by the river and lots of mud.'

'Oh!' Sheila looked dismayed. 'I hadn't thought of that. Usually, it is hot and sunny down here, isn't it?'

'Eventually, it will be. I checked the forecast. The rain is supposed to die out tomorrow morning. All the same, you'll need boots, jeans and so on. There's a good shop just down the road. Tell them where you are going and they'll kit you out.'

'That's thoughtful of you.'

The shrimps were served. As they began to eat, Sheila asked, 'What do you do for a living, Gene?'

'I'm a counsel at law. These shrimps are good, aren't they?'

'Delicious. A counsel at law? That sounds terribly important.'

'Yes, you could say that.'

'Are you on vacation?'

'Business and pleasure. I have to talk business with your husband.'

Sheila stiffened.

'Perry?'

'Yes. I expect he's told you he and Silas S. Hart are putting a movie together. I handle the legal work.'

Sheila felt a rush of cold blood down her spine.

'Silas S. Hart?'

'That's right. You look surprised. Mr Hart is my most important client.'

'I didn't know.' Sheila found the shrimps weren't so delicious.

That bastard Hart again! she thought. I'm sure he sicked that blackmailing investigator on me. *I should have thought you had other things to watch.* This handsome, smiling man had given her a warning! There could be no other explanation. All thoughts of sharing a bed with him this night vanished from her mind. Even if she had made advances, she was now sure he wouldn't have responded. She had only just missed a humiliating snub.

There was a steel hard core in Sheila that had dismayed her parents. From the moment she could talk, she had been difficult and obstinate. Her parents had been kindly people, and had shown great patience which Sheila had not appreciated. She would much sooner have a blazing row with them and have done with it. She really enjoyed fighting with Perry. A good, blazing row, and then to make up was the spice of life to her.

'Perry is at the fishing-lodge to find inspiration,' Franklin said as they finished the shrimps. 'Mr Hart is relying on him.'

'I'm sure.' There was a sharp note in Sheila's voice. 'Men with power always expect miracles.' She looked up to see Franklin, although still smiling, had a quizzical expression in his eyes.

There was a pause while a waiter cleared the dishes.

'I have some business to attend to tomorrow morning. That will give you time to do some shopping,' Franklin said. 'I suggest we have lunch together, then leave for the fishing-lodge immediately after. It is a good forty-mile drive.'

'All right.'

The main course was served with a flourish.

'Looks fine, doesn't it?' Franklin said, surveying his plate.

'It looks wonderful.'

They began to eat.

'So Perry isn't expecting you?' Franklin said, his voice casual.

Sheila's guard was up.

'He'll have a wonderful surprise.' She forked steak into her mouth. 'Hmm . . . good.'

'Sheila, I'm wondering if it was such a good idea for you to come all this way. You haven't even consulted Perry, have you?'

She gave him a cold, steady stare.

'Are you suggesting my husband won't be pleased to see me? And if you are, please tell me what business it is of yours.'

Franklin made a little grimace as if to imply this very young woman, seated opposite him, was going to prove more difficult than he had anticipated.

'Mr Hart was particularly anxious, Sheila, for your husband to get down to important work without interruption,' Franklin said quietly. 'That is the reason, and the only reason, why Perry has gone to his fishing-lodge . . . to be able to concentrate and work. Besides, Sheila, you couldn't have come at a worse time. You will find the conditions at the lodge disagreeable. I am told the footpaths are thick mud. It has been raining non-stop for the past three days. You will be cooped up in a small lodge and will distract Perry.' His smile appeared. 'As he doesn't expect you, don't you think it much more sensible for you to return to Long Island and leave Perry to work?'

Sheila finished the steak and began on the lobster.

'This crabmeat stuffing is fantastic,' she said.

'Oh yes. The fish food here is excellent. You haven't answered my question. Don't you think . . .'

'I haven't forgotten your question.' Her pretty face was hard. 'I should be glad if you wouldn't try to interfere with the lives of Perry and myself. I am sure you are acting under orders from Hart.'

'It's not a matter of interfering, Sheila. Perry has a big deal on. By being with him, you could destroy his creative thinking. You're very young. Perhaps you don't realise what a brilliant creative mind Perry has. He has been a tremendous success. There is a lot of money involved. By descending on him, you could ruin a very important deal.'

'And Silas S. Hart would be terribly upset?'

'So would Perry.'

'I don't think he would. I think he would be glad to have me with him. But as you appear to be so worried, Gene, I'll call him and let him settle this little argument.'

'That, of course would be the solution, but unfortunately I have already tried to contact him. His telephone is out of order.'

'Then let's change the subject,' Sheila said. 'I'll have a coffee.'

For the first time, Franklin lost his smile. Looking at him, she saw why he was Silas S. Hart's attorney. The grey eyes had suddenly turned to stone.

'What subject would you like to talk about, Sheila?' he asked, signalling to the waiter.

'Oh, anything.' She shrugged.

'So let's talk about you.'

The waiter cleared the dishes.

'Not a very interesting subject,' Sheila said.

'I think so. You see, Sheila, you are a very young woman. You are fortunate to be married to a rich, clever man. Would you want to lose him?'

The waiter placed the coffee before them.

'That's my business,' Sheila snapped, 'but if it will satisfy your curiosity, I won't lose him. Perry happens to love me. He has many possessions. I head the list.'

'Or do you just imagine you do?'

Sheila sipped her coffee.

'That's my business, and not yours.'

'I didn't want to bring this up,' Franklin said, 'but your husband has every reason and evidence to divorce you.'

Sheila's face hardened.

'Interesting.'

There was a long pause while she stared around the restaurant.

'Every reason and evidence to divorce you,' Franklin repeated. 'Now, please do what I suggest. I will drive you to the airport tomorrow. Go home.'

Sheila finished her coffee and stood up.

'I'm going to bed. You will drive me to Perry's lodge tomorrow. If you don't, I will find a way to reach him. Thank you for an excellent dinner. Shall we say midday tomorrow?'

'I wonder if you realise, Sheila, that you are behaving like a selfish, spoilt brat,' Franklin said quietly, looking up at her.

'Those were almost the same words my father used to say to me when *he* couldn't get his own way.' Sheila smiled. 'On second thoughts, I intend to find my own way to Perry's lodge. I will be leaving early, so don't wait for me. Is that understood?'

Franklin shrugged.

'I can't stop you. I do assure you, Sheila, Perry won't want a spoilt, selfish brat around when he is working.'

'We'll see.' Sheila leaned forward. 'I'll return the compliment, Mr Franklin. In spite of your good looks and your charm, you are a toady. You are frightened of Silas S. Hart. I'm sorry for you. I am not frightened of him. Goodnight,' and, turning, she walked out of the restaurant.

6

Using the Ross's spare bedroom, Hank Hollis slept until 10.00, knowing he would probably be up all night. After a shave and a shower, wearing his uniform, he came down to the living-room.

'I heard you moving around,' Mary called from the kitchen. 'Breakfast is ready. Sit down.'

Hollis sat at the laid table, and Mary brought in a pile of waffles which she set before him.

'You eat that. Eggs to follow,' she said, and returned to the kitchen.

Ten minutes later, she returned with a plate of three eggs and two thick slices of grilled ham.

She sat down opposite Hollis.

'How's the Sheriff?' he asked, pushing aside a few remaining waffles and starting in on the eggs.

'Hank, he's not getting any younger,' Mary said quietly. 'He's a big worry to me. He's been on the telephone since eight o'clock. He told me what you plan to do. He's worried. I'm worried. I don't think he'll ever forgive himself about Tom. Do you really think this man could be hiding in Mr Weston's lodge?'

'Look, Mrs Ross, this is police work. I've been trained to check out possibilities. There is a chance he could be there. I don't know.'

She nodded.

'Yes, I understand. Jeff wants to go with you. He keeps saying if he had gone with Tom, Tom might still be alive.'

'Frankly, Mrs Ross, I don't want him with me. He's not as young as I am. I've dealt with situations like this before.

He hasn't. You relax. He will be much more useful staying right here.'

'I told him that.'

Hollis finished one slice of ham and started on the other.

'I'll spell it out to him too. You cook a great breakfast, Mrs Ross.'

She put her plump, clasped hands on the table and looked directly at him.

'Hank, you will be careful.'

He grinned at her.

'Sure.' He looked out of the window. 'Well, the rain's stopped, and it looks as if the sun might come out.' He finished his breakfast, then pushed his plate aside. 'That was great.'

'I've prepared food for you,' Mary said. 'There's half a cooked chicken and lots of sandwiches. Jeff thinks you could be in the forest for quite a while.'

'That's terrific!' Hollis grinned again. 'Many thanks. I'll go talk to the Sheriff.'

'You really will be careful, won't you, Hank?'

'I'll be careful.'

He found Ross at his desk.

'Hi, Sheriff,' he said as he came in. 'Any news?'

'Sleep well? Mary fed you?' Ross asked, turning in his chair.

'Sure. What's the news?'

'Negative. I've talked to Jenner and Jacklin. There's no sign of Logan. I've called all the farmers: nothing there. It looks to me Logan did get away before the road-blocks were set up.'

'Unless he's holed up with Weston.'

'Yes.' Ross pulled at his moustache. 'Jacklin tells me he now has two hundred armed men on the hunt. Do you still think this man could be hiding with Weston?'

'As I said last night, I don't know. It's a hunch. I want to check.'

'I don't like you doing this on your own, Hank. I should be coming with you.'

'Don't let's go over this again, Sheriff. This is my thing.

Maybe nothing will come of it. I plan to climb a tree near Weston's place and sit and wait. That's not your neck of the woods. Leave it to me. I'll keep in touch on the radio.'

With a frustrated sigh, Ross nodded.

'I guess you're right. Well, okay, it's worth a try.' He got to his feet. 'I've checked your rifle. There's a walkie-talkie and a good pair of field glasses. Mary said she would provide food. What else do you want?'

Hollis stared at him for a long moment, then he said, 'I want to treat Logan as I once treated a murderous Vietnam sniper. If I see Logan, I want to shoot him. How do I stand?'

Ross shifted uneasily.

'That would be illegal, Hank.'

'I know, but who's going to prove he didn't shoot first?'

Ross rubbed his chin. He thought of the vicious murders of the Loss family. He thought of Tom Mason.

'So he shot first,' he said looking directly at Hollis. 'Okay. You spot him, then kill him. You have my backing all the way.'

Hollis grinned.

'That's all I want to know.' He moved over to where the rifle, the walkie-talkie and the field-glasses were lying. 'Then I guess I'll get off. Will you drive me to that turn-off road to Weston's place? From there on, I'll be on my own.'

Ross got to his feet.

'Let's go then.' He put his hand on Hollis's shoulder. 'For God's sake, Hank, take no risks. I don't want you to go the way Tom went.'

'I don't want that either,' Hollis said. His smile was grim. 'If I get a clear shot, I'll fix him, Sheriff. If I spot him and can't get a shot, I'll alert you, then we'll have to think how to get at him.'

Mary came in carrying the plastic sack of food.

'You're off, Hank?' Her plump face was strained and anxious.

'Many thanks, Mrs Ross.' Hollis patted her arm. 'Don't worry. It'll work out.'

The two men went out into the steamy sunshine and got in the patrol car.

At 09.00, Sheila, dressed and packed, leaving her suitcase in the motel lobby, crossed the street to Cab Calhoun's sport's outfitting store.

She had passed a restless night, and found the steamy heat from the early-morning sun unpleasant. Slight mist was rising from the sodden street. She entered the store, surprised at its size and its range of merchandise from fishing-tackle and sporting guns to clothes and footwear.

From behind a long counter, a tall, black man with a grizzled beard came to her, smiling.

'Morning, ma'm,' he said. 'I'm Cab Calhoun. Thank you for calling. What can I do for you?'

Sheila regarded this man and liked the look of him.

'You have quite a place here, Mr Calhoun.'

'I guess. It's taken me forty years to build it up. It's as good, if not better, than any other store you'll find in Jacksonville.'

'Congratulations.' A pause, then Sheila said, 'I am Mrs Perry Weston.'

Grizzled eyebrows lifted.

'Mr Perry Weston? Ah, sure. I well remember him. I had the pleasure to kit him out around three years ago. A fine gentleman if I may say so. I haven't seen him for too long.'

'I want to be kitted out too,' Sheila said. 'My husband is at his fishing-lodge. I am joining him. What do you suggest I buy, Mr Calhoun?'

'You want fishing-tackle?'

'No. Just sensible clothes.'

Calhoun smiled.

'That's no problem. You will want a half a dozen cotton shirts with long sleeves, a couple of pairs of jeans and two pairs of boots, then you're home.'

'Do you know where my husband's fishing-lodge is?'

'Why, sure.' Calhoun looked a little startled. 'But Mr Weston will be fetching you, I guess.'

'No. I'm giving him a surprise visit. I want to get there on my own.'

Calhoun scratched his beard.

'If you'll excuse me, Mrs Weston, that's setting yourself a tricky task. It's my business to keep in touch with the local road conditions. I know for a fact that the road leading down to Mr Weston's lodge is nearly washed out. If you would wait three or four days to give the road a chance to dry out, then there'd be no problem. I doubt if Mr Weston could make it now.'

'I intend to go there this morning,' Sheila said. 'I would be glad if you would tell me how to get there.' She smiled, a determined expression on her face. 'My father once told me that obstacles were made to surmount. I'm going this morning.'

Calhoun studied her, then nodded.

'Then I'll help you, Mrs Weston. I can find someone who will take you in a Jeep. That's the only transport that will get you there.'

'I'm going alone. I can handle a Jeep. Can I hire one?'

'Oh, sure. Okay, Mrs Weston, over there you'll find everything you want. You go ahead. I'll fix a Jeep for you.'

Forty minutes later, Sheila had selected the clothes she would need. Using a changing room, she put on a red and yellow cotton shirt, slid into tight-fitting jeans and put on heavy calf-high boots. Carrying her dress, picking up the bundle of clothes she had chosen, she went to the counter where Calhoun was drawing a map on a sheet of paper.

'All fixed, Mrs Weston?'

'Yes, thank you. You have a wonderful selection.'

'Well, now, m'am, I've got the Jeep fixed for you. It'll be around in ten minutes. Here's a map to tell you how to get to the lodge.' He pushed the sheet of paper towards her. 'You leave here, turn left onto the highway and drive around twenty miles. That'll be no problem. You'll come to a sign-post marked "River" on your left. Turn here. Now, here's where you will have problems. Take it slow. There'll be lots of mud and water, and I guess the Jeep

will get you through so long as you drive real slow. You'll
have around two miles of this road, then you'll come to
the river. Follow the road by the river and you will come
to Mr Weston's lodge. Just remember to let the Jeep take
you and don't force it.'

'Thank you, Mr Calhoun, you couldn't be more helpful.'

'Glad to oblige a determined young lady. Here are the
papers for the Jeep. Just needs your signature. It's for a
week's rental. Okay?'

Sheila signed the papers, then made out a cheque for
her purchases.

'May I ask you to give Mr Weston my compliments,
Mrs Weston?' Calhoun asked. 'Please tell him I hope to
see him soon.'

'Of course.' She held out her hand. 'Again many
thanks.'

'Want me to put your purchases in a suitcase for you?
You can return the case with the Jeep.'

'That'd be fine.'

By the time Calhoun had packed her clothes in a
battered suitcase, the Jeep arrived.

Carrying the suitcase, Calhoun followed Sheila from
the store to the Jeep where a black youth got out of the
driving-seat.

'I'll check out,' Sheila said, 'and collect my other
luggage.'

'You do that, m'am,' Calhoun said, then turning to the
black youth, he went on, 'Go, collect the lady's baggage,
Joel.'

As Sheila crossed the road, followed by the black
youth, a taxi pulled up outside the motel. Gene Franklin
came out of the motel, carrying a bulky briefcase. He
paused, seeing Sheila. She felt his eyes go over her and
saw his frown.

'Good-morning, Sheila,' he said. 'In spite of my advice,
I see you are going.'

She stared at him, her pretty face hard.

'Correct. I am still behaving like a selfish, spoilt brat,

Mr Toady,' and she walked by him into the lobby of the motel.

Franklin hesitated, then, shrugging, got into the taxi and was driven away.

While the black youth carried her suitcase and vanity-box to the Jeep, Sheila settled the motel check. Recrossing the street, she found Calhoun had put her luggage in the Jeep and was standing, waiting.

'Ma'm,' he said, 'this boy knows all the roads around here. He'll gladly drive you.'

Sheila smiled.

'Thank you, no. I'll be fine.' She shook hands. 'I'll tell my husband how very helpful you have been.' She climbed into the Jeep and started the engine.

'Just take it slow, m'am,' Calhoun said. 'It's been a pleasure to help you.'

Sheila gave him a wide, flashing smile and, with a wave of her hand, headed towards the highway.

Perry Weston came slowly awake and became aware that hot sunshine was streaming through the bedroom windows. He looked at his strap watch. The time was 08.30. Feeling hot and sticky, he got off the bed. He went to the door and found he was still locked in.

He stood still, listening, but heard no sounds of movement below. Going to the open window, he looked out onto the river, lit by the sun. He saw the road by the lodge was water-logged with thick, wet mud. Well, at least the rain had stopped and the sun was out.

Taking his time, he shaved, showered and dressed. He longed for coffee. If Jim Brown wasn't in control of this bizarre situation, he would get out his fishing tackle and spend the rest of the day by the river, but Jim Brown was in control.

Perry sat down, lit a cigarette and waited.

It wasn't until 10.00 by Perry's strap watch that he heard movements. Going to the door, he listened and heard Brown's tuneless whistling. Ten minutes later, he heard the key turn in the lock, and Brown entered.

Perry noted Brown was now wearing one of his long-sleeved shirts, hiding the tattooed snake on his arm. Brown looked relaxed as he gave Perry a mirthless grin.

'I've been catching up on sleep, Perry,' he said. 'You want breakfast? It's all ready.' While he was speaking, Brown's eyes were looking around the room, then he moved forward to the bedside table and picked up a big, silver-framed photograph of Sheila.

Perry watched as Brown studied the photograph, giving a nod of approval. He put the frame back on the table.

'Your girlfriend?' he asked.

'My wife,' Perry said curtly.

'Is that right? Nice. Lucky guy.' Brown shook his head. 'Some guys are lucky. I never found a girl I'd want to marry. You like married life?'

Perry got to his feet.

'I'd like a cup of coffee.'

He left the room and walked down the stairs to the living-room. He found the table laid. He sat down and poured himself a cup of coffee while Brown went into the kitchen. He returned in a moment, carrying two plates of thick, grilled ham.

'This freezer of yours, Perry, is sure something,' he said as he set one of the plates in front of Perry. He sat down. 'It's something to have money. I guess you have a pretty good setup in New York too.'

Perry began to eat. This man certainly could cook. The ham was done to a turn.

'It's okay. I live in Long Island.'

'Nice.' Brown was shovelling food into his mouth. 'Money can give you anything.'

'If you have enough of it. It depends what you want.'

'I'd like a wife like you've got,' Brown said. 'I've kicked around on my own in this fucking world too long. When I want a woman, I have to pick up some whore. I've never had a home, except the hole my father lived in. That was for the birds!'

'How long do you plan to stay here, Jim?' Perry asked.

'When the heat cools, I'll get moving. I've listened to the radio. The cops are still in an uproar.' Brown grinned. 'They won't find me here, that's for sure.' He looked up and stared at Perry. 'You're going to stake me. I'll want ten thousand. Okay?'

'It has to be okay, doesn't it?'

'You can say that again.' Brown finished eating and sat back. 'Yeah. We'll have to see how we fix it.'

'Where will you go, Jim?'

Brown shrugged.

'I'm good at fading out of sight. You don't have to worry about me. All you have to do is to worry about yourself.'

'Fading out of sight?' Perry said. 'For how long? Look, Jim, face facts. Wouldn't it be sensible to give yourself up? You can't go on running. Sooner or later, they'll catch up with you. Even in prison, you're alive.'

'You're talking like a goddamn priest.' There was a snarl in Brown's voice. 'Give myself up? Be locked away for the rest of my life? That's not for me. I'm not scared of death. No one is taking me alive.' His expression turned vicious. 'And I'll take as many cop bastards with me as I can.'

Perry was about to say something when the sound of the telephone bell startled him.

'Oh, yeah,' Brown said. 'I forgot to tell you. I've fixed the telephone. I'm a great little fixer. You answer, and, Perry, watch it.' He stared at Perry. 'I'm getting to like you, buster, so don't get tricky.'

Perry crossed to the telephone. He lifted the receiver.

'Who is this?' he asked.

'This is Mrs Grady, Rockville post office,' a woman said. 'I heard your telephone was out of order.'

'That's right. It's okay now. I guess it was the rain. It's working fine.'

'I was going to send Josh as soon as the road had dried out.'

'No need, Mrs Grady. Thanks for calling.'

'You're welcome, Mr Weston.'

Perry hung up.

'Checking the telephone.'

'I thought of that,' Brown said. 'Didn't want some guy coming here. Just be careful, Perry. Don't try using the phone. Right?'

'If it's okay with you,' Perry said, 'I'd like to start working. I came here to write a movie. What are you going to do?'

'Go ahead. Don't worry about me. I like this room. I'll watch TV. Know something, Perry? I feel real at home in this joint. I'll get lunch. There are a couple of juicy-looking pork chops in the freezer. Like that with French fried?'

'Fine,' Perry said and leaving the room, he walked down the short passage to his study. He sat at his desk and looked out of the window at the sun and the trees. He would have liked to be out with his fishing-rod. He leaned back in his chair and gave free rein to his imagination. After half an hour of concentrated thought, he took from his desk a block of paper and began to sketch out the first moves of the plot that just could please Silas S. Hart.

He became so absorbed in his work, he lost count of time. It was only when the door opened and Brown looked in that Perry was thrown back to reality.

'Chuck's up,' Brown said. 'Come and get it.'

Perry looked at his strap watch. The time was 13.00. He got to his feet and reluctantly left his desk, following Brown into the living-room.

A thick pork chop with a heap of French fried awaited him.

'Got no onions,' Brown said, sitting opposite Perry. 'I dig onions with pork chops.' He grinned mirthlessly. 'Can't have everything. My old man liked onions. I used to cook him fried onions and potatoes. He liked that. Meat, towards his end, wasn't all that good for him. He had rotten teeth.'

Perry cut into his chop, thinking everything this man said was now background for his plot.

'You were fond of your pa, weren't you, Jim?'

'Well, I guess. Know something? It's good to be fond of someone. He wasn't all that hot. Sometimes, I didn't think he liked me. There were times when he used to give me sly looks. I know looks. Okay, I was fond of him. It didn't matter how he felt about me. I had no one else, so I was fond of him. When I found him dead, something in my life went away.' He chewed, nodded. 'Damn fine meat.'

'How about your ma, Jim?'

Brown scowled.

'Don't talk about her. No good. You fond of your wife?'

'Of course.'

Brown nodded.

'I guess. Nice-looking girl.' He looked up. 'A bit young for you, isn't she?'

This ape of a man had touched a sensitive nerve. Perry winced.

'That's not your business, is it?' he said curtly.

Brown gave a sneering little grin.

'I guess that's right.' He eased back his chair. 'You working on a movie?'

'That's why I'm here.'

'How do you write a movie?'

Perry shrugged.

'If you want to know, you first get an idea. After you're sure the idea is sound, then you think of people to carry out the idea. Once you've created interesting people and the idea, the movie will more or less write itself.'

'Is that right? Sounds easy. The money's good, huh?'

'Nothing in this world is ever easy if it is to pay off, Jim.'

Brown studied him.

'You got characters?'

'I've just an idea.'

'What's the idea?'

'That's not your business either, is it?'

'I bet one of the characters is me.'

'If you think so, then think so.' Perry stood up. 'A great meal. I'll get back to my desk.'

Brown began to whistle tunelessly as he collected the plates. Back at his desk, Perry could still hear him whistling in the kitchen.

Sheriff Ross and Hank Hollis got out of the patrol car just before the turning down to the river. Silently, Ross handed the rifle to Hollis who slung it on his shoulder. He took the plastic sack of food and the radio transmitter. The two men looked at each other.

'Take no risks, Hank,' Ross said uneasily. 'I wish I were coming with you.'

Hollis grinned.

'Take it easy, Sheriff. I'll be in touch.'

'I'll never forgive myself if something happens to you,' Ross said.

'Cheer up!' Hollis grinned again. 'This is my speciality. Well, I'll get off. Don't worry about me.'

The two men shook hands, then Hollis moved onto the forest road. He waited until he heard the patrol car start up and drive away, then he began a slow, cautious walk, keeping to one side of the road. He unslung his rifle, hitched the plastic sack and the radio on his left shoulder and continued to move forward.

Once in the dense forest, he moved much more cautiously. He felt relaxed. This hunt after a vicious killer sent his mind back to the jungles of Vietnam. How often had he done this? Countless times! He had always come out alive, and a sniper dead. Okay, Chet Logan, you won't know what's going to hit you!

The road was fast drying, but in places there were pools of muddy water. Hollis skirted these, pressing against the wet shrubs. It took him over an hour to come within sight of the river. To his right, now no more than a couple of hundred yards away, was Perry Weston's fishing-lodge. Here, he warned himself, he must take the greatest caution. He moved back into the thickest part of the forest, using every bit of cover, moving so silently even the birds in the tree tops were not alarmed. Again, he moved forward, pushing shrubs gently aside, feeling thick mud on his boots. It was steamy hot and sweat ran down his face. His shirt and khaki slacks were wet from the soaking shrubs. Discomfort never bothered him. Once a jungle fighter, always a jungle fighter, his Captain had said to him. Damn right!

Another few yards, then parting the branches of a tree, Hollis found himself looking directly at the fishing-lodge. He stopped short, crouched and regarded the lodge.

There was no sign of life. He noted the curtains of the front windows were drawn. That didn't mean Logan wasn't somewhere either in the lodge or near the lodge, watching.

Hollis looked up at the tree. It seemed perfect for his purpose. Within reach were long foliage-covered branches.

Taking his hunting-knife from his belt, he cleaned off the thick mud from his boots, then, slinging the rifle, he caught hold of the lowest tree branch and began to climb.

He climbed slowly and carefully, taking care not to make movement among the branches. To him, it was an easy climb. He swung himself up and up, until he reached nearly to the top of the tree. From this vantage-point, he could look down at the fishing-lodge and still remain hidden.

Here, he paused. Two thick branches made a comfortable-looking fork. He nodded to himself, then settled, his legs astride a branch, his back against the thick trunk. So far, so good, he thought. I can stay up here for hours.

He hung the plastic sack of food on a branch, found a safe place for his rifle, then set the radio transmitter between his legs. He surveyed the fishing-lodge. Still no sign of life. This could be a waste of time, but he didn't think so. Why had the telephone cable been wrenched from its socket? That was the clue. That was the hint that Logan was hiding there with a gun on Weston. It was now a matter of patience, and Hollis had plenty of that.

By now, Hollis thought, the Sheriff would be back in

his office. He switched on the radio. Keeping his lips close to the transmitter, he said, 'Hollis. Are you hearing me?'

'Loud and clear, Hank,' Ross said.

'I've found a good tree, Sheriff. I can look right down at the lodge and can't be seen. There's no sign of life, but the front-window curtains are drawn. I guess I'll just have to wait.'

'You can get me whenever you want, Hank. I'm not moving from my desk. Keep in touch.'

'Over and out.' Hollis switched off the radio. He looked at his watch. The time was just after noon. Odd, he thought, Weston hasn't shown himself. One would have thought he would have come out. Maybe he had slept late and was now having a brunch, or maybe Logan was there and wouldn't let him out. Hollis decided to sample some of Mary Ross's sandwiches. He opened the plastic sack and found a big pack of ham and beef sandwiches and a bottle of water.

He ate two sandwiches, always keeping his eyes on the lodge. It would be good to have lit a cigarette, but that would be too dangerous.

He re-hung the sack, settled his back against the tree-trunk and relaxed to wait.

This was like old times, he thought. He thought of the most stubborn and dangerous sniper who was nearly, but not quite, as good as himself. This little Viet had con-cealed himself in a tree. From there, he had picked off two of Hollis's good friends. Hollis had sworn to get him. He had located where the shot had come from. In the hot, steamy darkness, he had climbed a tree within three hun-dred yards from the tree in which the sniper was con-cealed. He had waited for eighteen tense, nerve-stretching hours. That time, he had only two bars of soggy chocolate and his water-bottle, not like now with good sandwiches and half a chicken. Hollis nodded. It had been worth the wait. The jungle had been silent. Finally, the sniper showed himself. He shinned down the tree, lowered his trousers and squatted. Hollis had sent a bullet through his brain. The most satisfactory thing he had ever done in his Army career. And now he was up another tree, waiting to see if Chet Logan would appear.

Patience!

An hour crawled by. Then Hollis became alert. The grinding sound of a car engine in low gear approaching, made him peer forward.

To his startled surprise, he saw a Jeep moving slowly along the sodden river road. From his viewpoint, he couldn't see the driver. He unslung his rifle, watching as the Jeep slid on the muddy road, then he saw the Jeep pull up outside the fishing-lodge. He saw a blonde-haired girl, wearing a yellow-and-red shirt and tight jeans, jump out of the Jeep and walk up to the door of the fishing-lodge.

Oh, Hell! he thought. Here's a real complication! Who is this girl? What's she doing here? He pushed aside some foliage so he could get a better view.

She was knocking on the door. In the silence of the forest, Hollis could hear the impatient rapping of her knuckles.

He was now badly placed. He had only a half sighting of the front door. He saw it open. There was a long pause. Faintly he heard voices. It seemed to him, although he couldn't hear what was being said, there might be some kind of argument. Then he saw the girl push her way in and the front door slammed.

He switched on his radio.

'Sheriff?'

'I'm listening.'

It was a relief to hear Ross's steady, deep voice.

'There's a development here, Sheriff. A young girl has just arrived in a Jeep and she is now in the lodge. The Jeep belongs to Cab Calhoun, Jacksonville. Will you check?'

'Back in five minutes,' Ross said and switched off.

Hollis waited, staring down at the lodge. There was no sign of activity. Maybe, he thought, I was wrong. This killer isn't there. Weston had been expecting this girl. He could be sitting up in this tree with swarms of mosquitoes tormenting him for nothing.

118

But Hollis had learned to be patient. Still, letting the mosquitoes buzz around him, he watched and waited.

Ten minutes crawled by, then his radio came alive.

'Hank?' Ross's voice.

'I'm hearing you.'

'The girl is Perry Weston's wife. She hired the Jeep and told Cab she would be staying a week or so at the lodge. Look, Hank, I think you can come back. You're wasting your time. I am satisfied this killer did get away to Miami as Jacklin said. There's a massive hunt on for him. Come on back.'

'With respect, Sheriff, I'm not coming back yet. How do we know Logan isn't there? Okay, Mrs Weston could be on a visit. She could be walking into trouble. I'm staying and watching. How does anyone know that Logan is out of our district? I'm going to wait.'

'Yeah. Okay, Hank. Keep watch. I'll stay right here until you tell me you're coming back.'

'Over and out,' Hollis said and switched off.

When Sheila Weston turned off the Highway and began the descent to the river, she quickly realised that Cab Calhoun's warning she could have problems became a disagreeable fact.

Once Sheila had made up her mind to do something, nothing, no matter the difficulties, would deter her. She was determined to talk to her husband. When only ten years of age, she had driven her father's Jeep around his extensive ranch, much to the amusement and admiration of his cattle hands. She had heard one of the men say to another, 'That's a real hellion.' She had smiled with pride, as she was now smiling to herself, remembering those words.

So, okay, she was then a real hellion, and a hellion she would remain.

Skilfully, she manoeuvred the Jeep through the pools, the mud and the slime. She felt the steamy heat pressing down on her. She had taken the precaution to smear her face and hands with anti-mosquito cream so the buzzing swarm didn't bother her.

Eventually, she reached the big quagmire that had bogged down the Toyota. Seeing it, she stopped her crawl forward and stared at the mess of water and thick mud. Would the Jeep cope? If she got bogged down, she would be in real trouble. She got out of the Jeep and walked to the edge of the quagmire. She examined the ground. Either side of this swamp was firm ground. She nodded to herself. Returning to the Jeep, she engaged the four-wheel drive, edged the Jeep forward so the off-side wheels got a grip on the firm ground and moved forward, patiently taking her time.

The onside wheels sank into the quagmire, but the off-side wheels took hold. Holding her breath, feeling sweat running down her face and back, she slightly accelerated. She had to use all her strength to keep the Jeep from sliding. She could hear mud and water churning under her, then, with a jerk, the Jeep came through and she was clear.

While Sheila was continuing the drive down to the fishing-lodge, finding the road much easier now to cope with, the telephone bell rang on Grace Adams's desk.

With a work-load spread out on her desk, she snatched up the receiver with an impatient exclamation.

'What is it?'

'Mr Gene Franklin is calling, Miss Adams,' her secretary said. 'Okay to put him through?'

'Go ahead.'

There was a click, and Franklin came on the line.

'Hello there, Grace,' he said. 'I guess S. S. H. has left by now.'

'He's in Hollywood. What is it?'

'Bad news, I'm afraid.'

'That's something I could well do without!'

'Yes. Perry's wife is joining him at the fishing-lodge.'

'God almighty!' Grace exploded. 'How do you know?'

'It was the merest chance. I flew down to Jacksonville yesterday to get Perry to sign the contract and I ran into Sheila. She told me she intended to surprise Perry and spend a couple of weeks with him. I knew that this was the last thing S. S. H. would want. It was pouring with rain, so I arranged to put her up at my motel, gave her dinner, and for a nickel she would have jumped into bed with me. It looked fine until I began to sell her the idea she'd be wiser to leave Perry alone and go home, then she turned ugly. Nothing short of knocking her on the head and kidnapping her would have worked. No one, repeat no one, including S. S. H., can handle this obstinate little bitch.'

'So you're telling me she's with him?'

'She must be. The road conditions are bad. She rented a Jeep and left about half an hour ago. With luck, she could get bogged down, but it's my bet she will get to Perry.'

Grace Adams drew in a long, exasperated breath.

'You know what this means? There'll be no movie! With her bothering Perry, he won't do any work.'

'Why did the goddamn sucker marry that little bitch?'

'We won't go into that. I'll contact S. S. H. He'll love it!' and she slammed down the receiver.

Feeling triumphant, Sheila steered the Jeep along the narrow, mud-soaked road, driving slowly and carefully. Another ten-minutes' driving brought her in sight of the river. She smiled to herself. A hellion? Again she smiled. Obstacles were made to surmount! She nodded. How right! Then she saw the fishing-lodge. She recognised it from Perry's description.

Here I am, she thought, then unaware that she was being watched by Hollis perched in the tree, she steered the Jeep to the front door and cut the engine.

She sat for a long moment, looking at the lodge. Well, she thought, it is certainly primitive. It flashed through her mind whether she would be able to put up with living there for a couple of weeks. It would be utterly dull, utterly isolated. If she could not stand it, she told herself, she could drive to Miami where the bright lights always beckoned. But right at this moment she felt the need to have Perry's arms around her, to sit with him and talk about herself. He was the only one who would listen. All her women friends only half listened, waiting for a chance to jump in and tell her *their* troubles. Her men friends never listened. They nodded, smiled with sympathy and waited for the chance to tell her what great guys *they* were. But not Perry. He always listened and understood.

She jumped out of the Jeep and ran to the front door of the lodge. There was a heavy iron handle. What a surprise for Perry! she thought. She would take him to bed the moment she had had a bath. Then, lying in his arms, she would tell him about this bastard Hart and the private eye. She would even tell him about that awful Lucan.

She turned the door handle to find the door locked. She now saw the curtains were drawn at the three big windows.

Was Perry there? she wondered. God! What a flop if she had come all this way and he wasn't there!

She rapped on the door. Waited, then rapped again.

She heard the lock click back and her face lit up.

Perry!

The door opened.

The man she longed to talk to, the only man who understood and was kind to her stood before her.

The expression on his white drawn face sent a chill through her.

'Oh, God, no!' he exclaimed. 'Oh, Sheila! What are you doing here?'

His expression was something right out of a horror movie. It was all there: fear, terrible tension and despair.

'Perry, darling!' She rushed to him and threw her arms around him, hugging him. 'I know I shouldn't have come, but I needed you so much. Darling, tell me you are glad to see me!'

As she clung to him, over his shoulder, feeling his body trembling, she saw Jim Brown, standing just behind her husband, an evil smile on his face and a gun in his hand.

7

Perry felt fingers, like steel claws, clamp on his shoulders. With a violence he didn't think possible, he felt himself thrown aside. He thudded against the wall of the lobby. Sheila, still clinging to him, went with him. Together, they slid to the floor.

Jim Brown kicked the front door shut and pushed the bolts home. He moved away, his gun now back in its holster, and watched Perry and Sheila disentangle themselves and shakily stand up.

'What the hell is this?' Sheila shrilled. 'Who's this jerk? What's happening?'

More slowly, despair in his heart, Perry straightened up. He looked helplessly at Sheila, seeing her enraged expression, and he said quickly, 'Careful, darling. This man is dangerous.'

'You said it, buster,' Brown snarled. 'Now, this is your wife . . . right? She's stuck her pretty nose where it isn't wanted . . . right? So no tricks, buster.' He grinned evilly. 'You two could share a double funeral.'

With an effort, Perry composed himself.

'Okay, Jim. There'll be no tricks.'

Brown nodded.

'That's what I like about you, Perry. You're a guy I can deal with. Right. Take your wife in there and spell it out to her. I've things to do in the kitchen. You've got king-sized prawns. I'm good with them. We'll all have them for supper.'

'What is this?' Sheila screamed. 'Who is this man? What's going on?'

123

Perry gently took her arm.

'Let's go in and sit down, Sheila.'

'Don't baby me!' Sheila shrilled. 'Get rid of this man! I want to be alone with you! Get rid of him!'

Brown gave a barking laugh.

'She's real dumb, isn't she? Get her in there or I'll kick her in!'

The snarl in his voice scared Sheila. With a long look at him, she let Perry lead her into the big living-room. He sat by her side on the settee.

Brown appeared in the doorway.

'No tricks, Perry.'

'No.'

Brown nodded, then moved into the kitchen and out of sight.

'Perry! What is this?'

He put his hand on hers.

'Don't talk. Just listen. I am a hostage. Now you, coming here, are also a hostage. This man is being hunted by the police. He killed six people two nights ago. He is as dangerous and as vicious as a cobra.'

'Six people?' Sheila stared at him, her eyes round.

'Yes. Now, darling, please listen. He must be some kind of psychopath. The only way we can handle him is to be relaxed and nice to him. When I say nice, I mean don't say anything that could antagonise him. Do you understand?'

'Do you really mean . . . ?'

'Sheila! Be adult!' The snap in Perry's voice brought a flush to her face. 'This is deadly serious. This lunatic will kill us both if we provide him with the slightest excuse. For God's sake! Why did you come?'

The steel in her asserted itself. She stiffened, then looked directly at him.

'I came because I wanted to talk to you. I became sick of myself and the way I have been acting. I wanted to tell you so many things.'

'Okay. There'll be time for that. Right now, we both have to go along with this man or we'll finish up dead.'

They both paused to listen to Brown's tuneless whistle.

Perry moved close to her. He slid his arm around her shoulders as the door opened.

Brown came in.

'You told her, Perry?'

'I've told her.'

Sheila was regarding this man as he came in and shut the door. What an ape! she thought. Her eyes ran over his powerful body. His face which scared her, she disregarded, but his body! In spite of being scared, a thought came into her mind what it would be like to get into bed with a brute like this. She felt a tingle of sex run through her. She had never seen such a man. Those square, broad shoulders, the slim waist, those terrifyingly powerful hands!

'Okay,' Brown said. He looked at Sheila. 'You take it easy, baby, and we'll all get along nice. Right?'

Sheila nodded.

'You have a job to do, Perry,' Brown said. 'You're going right now to your bank and you're getting ten thousand bucks in cash, and you will chat up the jerks in the village and find out what the pressure is. Get it?'

Perry jumped to his feet.

'No! I'm not leaving my wife alone with you! That's for sure! I'm not going!'

Brown grinned.

'Yeah. That's what you think, but you'll go. Take a look at this.'

He looked around the room, then walked over to an occasional table and picked up a big, heavy pewter ashtray. He balanced it in his hands, staring at Perry.

'Watch, buster,' he said.

Effortlessly, as if the heavy ashtray was made of tin foil, he crumpled it, squeezed it and threw the ball of metal at Perry's feet.

'Let me tell you something,' Brown said softly. 'A couple of years ago, I hired a hooker for the night. She was young, but nothing like as pretty as your wife. She wanted ten bucks. I had ten bucks, so we went back to her pad and I gave her ten bucks. Then a big black buck appeared and told me to get the hell out. That was putting pressure on me. I told you when people put pressure on me, I hit back. That's natural, isn't it? So this big black buck put pressure on me and I hit him. I broke his goddamn neck. The hooker began to scream so I fixed her. I took her head in my hands and squeezed.' He paused to look at Sheila. 'You'd better listen, baby. Okay, I squeezed. Know what happened? Her brains came out of her ears. When I squeeze, I squeeze good.'

Sheila shuddered, staring up at Perry who had turned white.

'That's it, buster,' Brown snarled. 'From now on you do exactly what I say otherwise I'm going to take your babe's head in my hands and I'm going to squeeze her face like some rotten orange. Okay?'

'Perry!' Sheila, now terrified, shrilled, 'Do what he says!'

Perry looked around for a weapon. With the courage of despair, with the normal instinct of a man who must protect his mate, he grabbed up a pathetically fragile glass vase and threw himself at Brown.

Grinning, Brown avoided his clumsy rush and cuffed him with his open hand. The cuff sent Perry reeling. Dropping the vase, which smashed to pieces, he lost his balance and landed on the settee.

'Nice try, buster. Next time I'll use my fist,' Brown said. 'Then you'll know what it is to be hit. You going or am I going to break your neck and squash your babe's face?'

Sheila gave a soft scream, then put her hands to her mouth. Perry shook his head. The slap had stunned him. He knew it was just a slap, but the force of it horrified him. He remembered this ape of a man lifting the car clear of the quagmire. This brutal, ape-like strength was beyond imagination.

'Now, listen, Perry,' Brown said. 'You're scared I'm going to screw your wife as soon as you go.' He nodded. 'That's something I can understand. You go. I'm not going to touch her. We'll sit here and wait for you to come back with the money. Play straight with me, and I'll play straight with you. Get the money, find out what the pressure is, and you don't need to worry about your wife. That's a promise. Okay?'

'You'll leave her alone? You won't touch her?' Perry said getting unsteadily to his feet.

'So long as she sits still, doesn't make trouble, I don't touch her, but if she gets tricky she'll get a slap.' Brown grinned. 'Fair enough?'

Listening, Sheila felt a powerful sexual urge sweep through her. Looking at this man, she imagined him taking her. She imagined him entering her. She imagined gripping those terrifyingly muscular shoulders.

'Sheila, darling, I'll have to go,' Perry said. 'If Jim tells me he won't touch you, I'm prepared to trust him. Now, for God's sake, do just what he says . . . please.'

Sheila forced a smile.

'I will. Before you go, I would like my baggage. Would you get the two bags?'

Looking at her, Perry felt a qualm. She had now completely relaxed. Her eyes had lit up. She was once more the Sheila he had had to cope with since they had married.

'Get her bags, Perry,' Brown said.

Hollis, in his tree-top, watched Perry come out into the steamy hot sunshine. He watched Perry take two suitcases from the Jeep, then return to the lodge.

'Honey, please take them to our room,' Sheila called.

Perry carried the bags up the stairs. Brown sat down, staring thoughtfully at Sheila who was smiling.

Perry came down the stairs and stood in the doorway of the living-room.

'Okay,' Brown said. 'Get the money. While you're down there, get some onions and eggs. Fill the Jeep with gas. When I shove off, I'll use the Jeep. Okay?'

'Yes.' Perry looked at Sheila. 'Darling, it'll take a couple of hours. Please remember what I've said.'

'Of course.' She smiled. 'I'm not scared. If Jim says he won't touch me, why should I be scared?'

Perry hesitated, then nodded and went out to the Jeep.

Hollis watched Perry get into the Jeep, turn it and head

towards the river road, leading to the highway. He switched on his radio.

'Sheriff?'

'Hearing you.'

'A new development. Weston has just gone off in the Jeep, heading for Rockville. The road's still bad, but in the Jeep he'll get there. His wife is in the lodge. What do you make of it?'

'Could be okay. I don't know. I'll be on the look out for him when he arrives.'

'I don't think it's okay. I still think Logan is now holding a gun on Mrs Weston. I'm sticking. Keep in touch,' and Hollis switched off.

As soon as Sheila heard the Jeep start up and drive away, she smiled at Brown.

'I guess I have to ask your permission, Jim,' she said. 'I would like to unpack and take a bath.'

Brown studied her, then nodded.

'Go ahead, but no tricks, baby. Right?'

'Will you cut out calling me baby?' Sheila said, getting to her feet. 'My name is Sheila.'

'Go take a bath, baby,' Brown said. 'Just no tricks.'

Sheila left the living-room and climbed the stairs to the double bedroom. She stripped off, ran a bath, then sank into the warm water.

What an ape of a man! she thought, feeling an uncontrollable sex urge run through her. So he won't touch me! She released a soft laugh. It would be fun to seduce him. Marvellous to lie beneath him. All the other men, including Lucan, didn't compare with this brute. She had two hours!

She remained only for a few minutes in the bath, then she dried herself and went to the big mirror and fixed her hair. She then went into the bedroom, naked, and unlocked her suitcase. She found a flimsy, transparent wrap which she put on. She closed and relocked the suitcase.

She found her heart was thumping and she was breathing fast.

128

Now, she thought, the big seduction scene! She giggled, feeling lust move through her. She went to the door and called, 'Jim! I can't get my suitcase open. Come up, please, and fix it for me.'

She moved to the big bed and waited. She had her back to the sunlit window and knew the light was shining through her flimsy wrap. No man, she told herself, could resist this temptation, let alone an ape like Brown.

Brown appeared in the doorway, his blunt features expressionless.

'Sorry to bother you, Jim. I'm an idiot with locks,' Sheila said, giving her most seductive smile.

'Is that right?' Brown said, still remaining in the doorway. She was aware he was eyeing her near-naked body. She felt moisture gathering in her loins.

As he still remained motionless, she said impatiently, her voice a little shrill, 'We haven't much time. Don't just stand there!' She opened her wrap so he could see her body. 'Come to me!'

'You deaf or something?' Brown said. 'Didn't you hear I told Perry if he played straight with me, I'd play straight with him? Are you a goddamn dope? Now, I'll tell you something. To me, you are no better than the worst hooker I've ever screwed. You are, to me, like the mess a dog leaves on the sidewalk. Even if I hadn't told Perry I wouldn't touch you, I wouldn't now touch you!' Turning, he moved to the head of the stairs, slamming the door behind him.

Perry Weston drove down Rockville's main street and pulled up outside the bank. The time was now 15.00. There were few people on the street. Most of the citizens had done their shopping, and he was thankful that only the old were sitting in the shade of the trees, dozing or boring each other with small talk.

He entered the bank which was deserted except for an elderly woman, seated behind the counter, making entries in a ledger. She looked up, stared, then smiled.

'It's Mr Weston, isn't it?'

'That's right. Mr Allsop around?'

'Why, of course.' She slid her bulk off the stool. 'I'll get him, Mr Weston.'

Fred Allsop, the manager of the bank, a small, thin man in his late fifties, came bustling out of his office.

'Why, Mr Weston! What a pleasure!' He shook hands. 'You are here for a vacation?'

Perry was continually thinking of Sheila. Could he trust this ape of a man? He must get back as quickly as he could.

'Well, no. I'm on a trip, Mr Allsop. I need money. I'm in a hurry.'

'Mr Weston, we are here for service. We haven't seen you for a long time. What can I do?'

'I want ten thousand dollars in one-hundred-dollar bills.'

Allsop blinked.

'Well, you haven't that amount in your account, Mr Weston. That's quite a sum.'

With an effort, Perry controlled his impatience.

'I need the money, Mr Allsop!' he said, his voice sharp. 'If you want, call my New York bank. I'm in a hurry!'

Startled by the bark in Perry's voice, Allsop said hurriedly, 'I'll arrange it, Mr Weston. Ten thousand in one-hundred-dollar bills?'

'That's what I said! I have some shopping to do. I'll be back in a quarter of an hour. Okay?'

'Yes, Mr Weston.'

These small-time bankers! Perry thought as he left the bank and crossed over to the self-service store. As he entered, Sheriff Ross moved across the street from his office and walked into the bank.

'Fred,' he said. 'What did Mr Weston want?'

Allsop hesitated.

'Well, Jeff, maybe it's not your business, but if you want to know, he's asking for ten thousand dollars in one-hundred-dollar bills.'

'Can you stall?'

Allsop looked startled.

'I told him I'd fix it. He was most insistent. Why? What's going on?'

'Never mind, Fred. Give him the money,' and leaving Allsop staring in bewilderment, Ross, worried, moved across the street and leaned against the wooden rail outside the self-service store.

Perry bought a dozen eggs, two lettuces and a small sack of onions. As he came out into the steamy sunshine, he saw Ross. His heart skipped a beat as Ross came to him with an outstretched hand.

'Shopping, huh?' Ross said. 'Nice to see you around, Mr Weston.'

Perry shook hands.

'Yeah. It's great to be back. Nice to see you again.' Then remembering Brown's orders to find out what the pressure was, containing his impatience to return to the fishing-lodge, he went on, 'Got a little business with the bank. Suppose we have a beer together, Jeff?'

'Sure. I'll be over at Tom's bar,' Ross said, and nodding, he started down the street.

Perry put his purchases in the Jeep and then entered the bank.

'All ready for you, Mr Weston,' Allsop said. 'Just sign here.'

Perry signed the form and picked up the bulky envelope.

'Many thanks. Your service is terrific.' He shook hands, then, leaving the bank, he locked the envelope away in the Jeep, then walked down the street to Tom's bar.

This was a bar which he had frequented a number of times when he had first moved into the fishing-lodge. The fat, jovial-looking barman beamed at him as he entered.

'Mr Weston! My pleasure!'

'Nice to see you again, Tom,' Perry said and shook hands. He looked around. There were only a few men sitting at tables at this hour, but all recognised him. They touched their hats, nodding a welcome. Perry saw Sheriff Ross sitting at a corner table.

'Two beers, Tom,' Perry said and crossed the room, forcing a smile for each man who was giving him a welcome. He sat by Ross's side.

Ross eyed him. He could see Perry was tense.

'I can't stay long,' Perry said as Tom brought the beers. 'I have my wife with me. I don't want to leave her too long alone.'

'I guess.' Ross sipped his beer. 'All okay at the lodge?'

'No problems.' Perry stared at the beer in his glass. No problems? What an understatement!

'Mary was wondering if you need her, Mr Weston,' Ross said. 'As soon as the road dries out, she could come down and clean up for you.'

'No, thanks. My wife can handle it. Give Mary my love.'

'Sure will.' Ross nodded. 'You writing a movie?'

'Yep.' Perry forced himself to sound casual. 'This killer. He gave me an idea. Any news of him? Has he been caught?'

'No. There's a big man-hunt on for him.' Ross leaned back in his chair. 'The police believe he is now somewhere in Miami,'

'Do you think he'll get away?'

'He'll give us a run for our money, Mr Weston, but sooner or later, we'll catch up with him.'

'I guess so.' Perry sipped his beer. He desperately wanted to confide in this big, calm-looking man, but he knew that if there was police action he and now Sheila would be the first to die. 'I'm working on this idea, Jeff. It was you coming to my place checking to see if this killer was hiding in one of the fishing-lodges that sparked me off.'

'Is that right, Mr Weston?' Ross remained relaxed in expression, but mentally very alert. 'I guess that happens to men with your imagination.'

'When you and your deputy left, I thought what would happen if this man was hiding in my place. From what you told me he is a nut-case and very dangerous. I tried to imagine how I would react if he appeared with a gun.'

Perry paused to sip his beer, then forced a laugh. 'It began to intrigue me.'

'Sure. I see that. What did you imagine, Mr Weston?'

Perry hesitated. Was he talking too much? He knew Ross was no fool, but what he had said so far must be acceptable without causing Ross to call out the National Guard.

'Quite a situation for a movie,' he said, lighting a cigarette. 'But I saw it would be static. You know? A criminal and a writer holed up in a lonely fishing-lodge. So far so good, but then what? Then the writer's wife arrives. He didn't expect her. Now the plot comes alive. This man now has two hostages. That's a big step forward. I'm still working on the idea.'

'Sounds fine to me,' Ross said. 'Yeah. I've seen all your movies, Mr Weston. This one could be the tops.'

'Glad you think so.' Perry finished his beer. 'The trick now is how to finish the movie. You see these two are hostages. If the police come to the rescue, the killer will kill them, then fight it out until he himself is killed. I can't allow this to happen. This might not work out.'

Ross was now convinced that Chet Logan was hiding in Weston's lodge, but he gave nothing away as he too finished his beer.

'I could make a suggestion, Mr Weston. Of course, I'm not in your trade. I'm thinking as a cop.'

In spite of trying to be casual, Perry slightly stiffened, and Ross, watching him, saw his reaction.

'Any idea is better than none,' Perry said. 'What's the suggestion, Jeff?'

Ross thought for a long moment, then said, 'The setup is your character has a homicidal killer in his lonely fishing-lodge?'

How right! Perry thought, but merely nodded.

'Two cops arrive. Your character knows if he gives them the nod, there'll be a shoot-out. Right?'

Again Perry nodded.

'These two cops suspect what is happening. They can see your character is in danger so they leave as Hollis and

I left. Now, suppose the younger cop happens to have served in the Marines as an anti-sniper. Suppose he returns to the scene, climbs a tree, overlooking the lodge, and waits.'

Perry drew in a long, slow breath. He realised that Ross knew Brown was hiding in his lodge. He thought of Hank Hollis: lean, tough, every inch an ex-marine. Was he really already up a tree, watching?

'Sounds good,' he said, aware his voice was husky. 'Then what?'

'Well, here is a tricky situation, Mr Weston, but I guess with your know-how and for a movie, you could get around it.'

'So?'

Now it was Ross's turn to hesitate, then, shrugging, he went on, 'This killer had murdered six people in one night. If he is caught, he'll go away for thirty years which doesn't mean a damn. He could be paroled after serving only eight or less years so he'd be loose again to kill more innocent people. The cop up the tree would treat this killer as he treated murderous Viet snipers. That's against the law, Mr Weston. As cops, we must arrest this man for trial, but this cop isn't going to bother his head about that. So he kills this man.'

Perry stared down at his hands.

'I don't think that would jell, Jeff. It would put the police in a bad light.'

'Sure, but you could think up some solution. Suppose this killer spots the cop and fires at him, then the cop is justified in killing him.'

Perry felt a cold chill run through him.

'I understand.'

'There's another trick you will have to think up, Mr Weston,' Ross said quietly. 'Your character and no one else can do it. Your character has to find a pretext to persuade the killer to show himself . . . to come out into the open so the cop in his tree can nail him. It's got to be a certain shot. If the cop fires and misses, the killer will dive for cover and your character and his wife are as good as dead, so somehow you have to think up an idea for your character to entice the killer out into the open.'

Perry thought of Brown. *Entice him out into the open.* What plausible reason could he give Brown to persuade him to show himself?

Watching him, Ross saw his look of despair.

'Think about it, Mr Weston,' he said. 'There's no other way.'

'Yes.' Perry abruptly stood up. 'I must be getting back. This has been a very helpful talk, Jeff. Thanks.'

Ross got to his feet and the two men shook hands. They stared at each other for a long moment, then Perry walked across the road to the Jeep.

Hank Hollis eased his position as he straddled the thick branch of the tree.

A depressing thought struck him. Fifteen years ago, when he was twenty-five years of age, he had thought nothing of hiding in a tree in steamy heat, watching and waiting, but now, after five hours of waiting, he realised he wasn't the man he once was. His back was aching. His crotch was getting sore. The mosquitoes tormented him. All this he had laughed off fifteen years ago. He remembered once a snake coming along the branch where he was sitting. He hadn't moved. He knew one movement from him would alert the Viet sniper who was also watching. He had let the snake slide over his legs and disappear into the foliage. He was damn sure he wouldn't have remained still now. Fifteen years was a long time! Although he attended the rifle club twice a week, and was reckoned to be the best shot there, he knew his snap-shooting wasn't as sharp as it once was. He looked at his watch. The time was 16.25. In another three hours it would be dusk, then quick darkness. Then what? Would Logan show himself? Hollis decided he couldn't remain up the tree during the night. As soon as it was dark, he would climb down, move into the forest and sleep. Then, before dawn, he would climb the tree and wait.

Then he heard a soft bleep from his radio and switched
it on.

'Sheriff?'

'Yup.' Ross's voice was soft. 'I'm now damn sure that
Logan is in the lodge. I've been talking to Weston.'
Briefly, he described the conversation he had had with
Perry. 'Weston is in a tight situation, Hank. So long as
Logan remains out of sight, there's nothing we can do for
either Weston or his wife. I could call out the National
Guard and have the lodge surrounded, but that would
mean Logan would murder the Westons. Weston is
smart. He has ideas. He could persuade Logan to show
himself. Then it's up to you.'

Hollis wiped the sweat off his face.

'I'm with you, Sheriff.'

'It looks as if Logan is going to make a break for it.
Weston drew ten thousand dollars from his bank. Logan
could take off when it's dark, but I'm sure he will kill
both the Westons before he goes. He wouldn't want them
to raise the alarm that he is on the move. This is a real
mess, Hank.'

'Yeah. Okay, I'll keep watch.'

'I guess I should come down there and relieve you.'

'No! This is my problem. Not yours. I'll handle it.'

Hollis heard Ross sigh.

'How are you making out, Hank? You've been up that
tree for more than five hours.'

Hollis hesitated, then decided he wasn't going to get
Ross in a flap. The last thing he wanted was this big,
bulky man pushing his way through the forest and
alerting Logan.

'I'm fine,' he said. 'Don't worry about me, Sheriff. This
is my speciality. I'll keep in touch. Tell Mrs Ross her
sandwiches were great.'

'Okay. Keep alert. Let me know when Weston gets
back,' and Ross switched off.

The next hour dragged by. Hollis kept shifting his
position. He looked down at the glittering river and
longed to take off his sweat-soaked clothes and take a

swim. To pass the time he ate some of the cold fried chicken. He was thirsty and longed for a beer. He also longed for a cigarette.

Show yourself, you bastard! he thought. Come on! Show yourself!

But there were no signs of life from the lodge. Yes, he was right. Logan must be there, otherwise, on this hot evening, Weston's wife would have come out. Hollis imagined her, terrified, cooped up with a thug like Logan.

Then he heard the sounds of the Jeep approaching. He became very alert. He saw the Jeep pull up outside the lodge and watched Perry get out. Perry took from the hatch back a sack of shopping and he saw the front door open. Perry entered and the door shut.

Hollis switched on the radio.

'Sheriff?'

'Listening.'

'Weston's back. He's left the Jeep outside the entrance.'

'Okay. Keep alert, Hank,' and Ross switched off.

Brown, his face a hard, suspicious mask, had his gun in his hand.

'Shut and bolt the door, Perry. Put the sack down. Now turn around. No tricks!'

Perry did as he was told and felt Brown's powerful hands run over his body.

'Okay,' Brown said. 'Now I'll take a look at the sack. I never take chances. If there'a a gun in it, you're dead!'

With a swift movement, he upended the sack and surveyed its contents, then he grinned at Perry.

'You're smart. Onions, huh? You like onions?'

'Where's my wife?' Perry said.

'No problem. She's upstairs, unpacking. I said you play straight with me and I'll play straight with you. Let's talk.' Holstering his gun, he walked into the living-room. 'What's the news?'

Perry followed him and sat down.

'I've got the money. Ten thousand in one-hundred-dollar bills.'

'Man! Aren't you smart!' Brown said, leaning against the wall. 'What's the pressure like?'

'I talked to the Sheriff. The search for you has shifted to Miami. There *is* no pressure here.'

Brown stared at him.

'This straight?'

With an effort, Perry kept his face expressionless.

'Straight.'

'Did you talk to the Deputy?'

'No.'

'Did you see him?'

Here it is, Perry thought, sure that the lean, tough-looking Deputy was the man up in the tree, overlooking the lodge. He took out a pack of cigarettes.

'I saw him,' he lied. 'He was doing something to the patrol car. I didn't speak to him.'

'Straight?' There was a snap in Brown's voice.

Perry lit the cigarette.

'Straight.'

'The Sheriff is nothing, but that Deputy . . .' Brown rubbed his chin. 'So, okay, the pressure's off. Right?'

'Yes.'

'Where's the money?'

'In the Jeep.'

Brown's eyes narrowed.

'Don't sit there! Go, get it! I want to see what ten thousand dollars in one-hundred-dollar bills look like.'

Perry had never ceased to marvel at the speed of thought. In that split second, as he stared up at Brown, a thought flashed into his mind. Suppose he told Brown to get the money himself? Suppose Brown, anxious to lay his hands on the money, thoughtlessly went out to the Jeep?

Find a pretext to get him out into the open.

'Hear me?' Brown snarled. 'Go, get it!'

No, Perry thought. It would be far too dangerous to tell this man to get it himself. Looking at Brown, seeing the suspicious gleam in his eyes, Perry decided Brown wouldn't go, and, what was more, he would begin to distrust him. If he was to get Brown into the open, he would have to think of a much more subtle method.

He got slowly to his feet, crushed out his cigarette, then walked to the door.

'I'll get it.'

Brown followed him to the front door, his gun now in his hand. He drew the bolts.

'No tricks, Perry,' he said. 'Hurry it up!'

Hollis, in his tree, heard the bolts being drawn. He snatched up his rifle, ready for action. Then seeing Perry come hurriedly out of the lodge to the Jeep, he muttered a curse.

Was Logan never going to show himself?

He watched Perry return to the lodge, a big, bulky envelope in his hand. The money, of course, he thought. Well, this could be the start of something. But suppose Logan took off when it was dark? He would have to stay alert from now on. There would be no question of sleep.

Cradling the rifle, he leant his aching back against the tree and waited. Half an hour crept by. At least the mosquitoes seemed bored with tormenting him, and it was turning cooler. What he would give for a cigarette!

Then something happened which he wished would never have happened. He heard a rustle in the undergrowth that stiffened him to attention, his hands gripping the rifle. Then a dog began to bark.

He peered down, but the tree foliage was so thick he couldn't see the ground.

He could hear the dog snarling and barking at the foot of the tree. Then he heard a man call out, 'Found something up there, Jacko? Come on! You ain't no tree-climber!'

With sweat running down his face, Hollis raised himself. He could see a tall, thickset man, a fishing-rod in his hand, by the river.

The dog continued to bark savagely.

Hollis remained motionless. What a goddamn giveaway, he thought. Logan must hear the dog!

The man called again, a snap in his voice. 'Jacko! To heel!'

The dog abruptly stopped barking and joined the man on the river path. The man bent and patted the dog, and the two moved on, passing the lodge. For a moment, the man paused to stare at the parked Jeep, then went on, the dog obediently following him.

As Perry returned to the lodge, Brown snatched the envelope from his hand and slammed and bolted the door.

'Ten thousand dollars, huh?' Brown grinned at Perry. 'Man! You're smart!'

He moved into the sitting-room.

'I want to talk to my wife,' Perry said. 'You count the money, Jim. Just make sure I haven't cheated you.'

Brown's steel-like fingers closed on his arm.

'Plenty of time, Perry,' he said. 'You have a lifetime to talk to your wife. She's okay. You played straight with me. I told you I'd play straight with you. I want to talk to you.'

Knowing resistance would be dangerous, Perry went with him into the living-room. He watched as Brown spilled out the bills on the table.

'Man! Money!' Brown muttered. 'The most beautiful sight in the world!' He pushed the bills around with a thick finger. 'I've never seen so much money.' He turned and grinned at Perry. 'You're smart, Perry.'

'I want to talk to my wife,' Perry said quietly.

'Sure. You said that before.' Brown began to gather up the bills, pushing them into the envelope. 'Okay, sit down. I want to go over this again.'

Containing his impatience, Perry sat down and lit a cigarette. Brown sat opposite him, the envelope in his hand.

'Go over what again?' Perry asked.

'You saw that old fart of a Sheriff . . . right?'

'I saw him.'

'And he told you the cops are now looking for me in Miami . . . right?'

'Yes.'

'He said the pressure was off . . . right?'

'That's what he told me.'

140

Brown stared directly at Perry, his vicious eyes probing.
'You believed him?'

'I had no reason not to,' Perry said, aware his mouth
was turning dry.

Brown nodded.

'The pressure's on around Miami . . . right?'

'So the Sheriff told me.'

'No pressure here, huh?'

Perry thought of the cop up in the tree, watching the
lodge. He dragged on his cigarette and slowly released the
smoke.

'That's what the Sheriff said.'

'You'd know, wouldn't you, Perry?'

'I only know what he told me.'

'He wouldn't lie to you, would he, Perry?'

Perry felt sweat trickling down his spine.

'We're good friends, Jim. There's no reason for him to lie
to me.'

'Although we ain't good friends, Perry, you wouldn't lie
to me either?'

At this moment the telephone bell rang.

Brown stiffened. Automatically the gun jumped into his
hand.

'Answer it, but be careful. No tricks.'

Perry got to his feet and lifted the receiver.

'Is that Perry?' A man's voice.

'Yes. Who is this?'

'Gene Franklin. I've been trying to contact you. Your
phone was out of order. How are you?'

Perry drew in a deep breath. Keeping his voice steady,
he said, 'I'm fine.' He was aware of Brown pointing a gun
at him. 'Long time no see. How are you?'

'Fine. I'm at Jacksonville. I've got a contract I want to
talk to you about. Suppose I drive over or maybe you can
come up here?'

'Sorry, Gene. You've interrupted. I'm getting this script
together. I don't want to leave it. The contract will have to
wait.'

'Sure, I understand. Well, I guess it can wait, but S. S. H.
wants it signed.'

'He'll have to wait too.' There was a snap in Perry's voice.

'I met your wife at Jacksonville. She's with you, isn't she?'

'Yes.'

A pause, then Franklin said, 'S. S. H. wouldn't approve. She'll be a distraction.'

If this situation hadn't been so desperate, Perry would have laughed. Distraction? How about a vicious killer sitting, pointing a gun at him?

'I write scripts for Mr Hart, but neither he nor anyone else dictates my private life,' Perry said. 'See you later, Gene,' and he hung up.

Brown returned the gun to its holster.

'That's telling them, Perry,' he said and grinned. 'You're smart.'

'You finished, Jim? I want to talk to my wife.'

'Sure. You seem to have your wife on your nut. She's okay. I want to tell you something. When it's dark, I'm taking off,' Brown said. 'You'll like that, won't you? I'll take the Jeep. No cop has ever caught me, and no cop ever will. I'll take off.'

Perry passed his hand over his sweating face.

'Can't say I'll be sorry, Jim,' he said, and forced a smile. 'This has been an experience.'

'I guess.' Brown leaned back in his chair. 'One thing, Perry. Listen good. I like you. You're smart, and you've been straight with me. Watch that wife of yours. Man! She needs watching. Know her problem? She has red-hot pants. If she was my wife, I'd beat the hell out of her. I'm being straight with you. It's not my business, but I'm telling you.' He rolled up his sleeve to reveal the cobra tattooed on his arm. 'I'd trust her as I'd trust this snake. Okay?'

As Perry began to protest, both men heard the loud, savage barking of a dog.

142

8

For more than an hour Sheila lay on the big double bed, Brown's words burning into her mind, over and over again:

To me, you are no better than the worst hooker I've ever screwed. You are, to me, like the mess a dog makes on the sidewalk.

At first, tears of humiliation ran down her face. Then the shock of sexual frustration, then, finally, a cold rage. Her body stiffened, her fists clenched.

No man had ever dared to speak to her like this!

You ape! God! You stinking animal!

She swung her legs off the bed and stood up. The rage engulfing her left her breathless. She hammered her clenched fists together. Her body was shaking.

No man would ever speak to her like that and get away with it!

You are, to me, like the mess a dog makes on the sidewalk.

Me!

Sheila began to move slowly around the room.

After some five minutes, she gained control of herself, but her rage against Brown burned. Her breathing eased, and she began to think. She sat down and stared at the sunlit window.

I'll fix you, you ape, she told herself. Somehow, I'll fix you!

How can I? she thought, but I'll do it if it's the last thing I ever do! Mushy thinking. I want to see you dead! How? A good question. She thought of the telephone. The police! Then she realised this was still mushy thinking. She would never get near the telephone. This ape was in control!

Wait a few minutes. Get control of yourself, she thought. She got up and went into the bathroom. She bathed her face in cold water. She looked at herself in the mirror, aware that the steel in her was exerting itself. She was now relaxing. She spent some minutes fixing her face, then satisfied, she returned to the bedroom and opened the suitcase Calhoun had lent her. She selected a fresh shirt and another pair of jeans and dressed. All the time her mind was active. Her thoughts were only on Brown. How to fix him?

Now, almost calm, she sat in a lounging-chair. Her mind darted like a field-mouse collecting food.

Finally she nodded, now completely calm.

Nothing else will do. I must kill him!

She sat still, repeating the thought again in her mind.

Yes! But how?

She thought of his brute strength. The way he had crushed the pewter ashtray. The way he had slapped Perry.

If only she had a gun!

Then she stiffened and sat up straight.

A gun!

She had a gun!

How could she have forgotten?

She remembered taking Perry's gun from the safe and scaring the life out of that stinking private eye. She remembered stuffing the gun into her handbag.

She jumped to her feet.

Where was the handbag? She looked at the two suitcases. She looked around the room, her eyes searching.

No handbag.

Then she remembered. She had put the handbag in the Jeep's map pocket by the driver's seat when she had left Jacksonville. Perry had missed it. So, the handbag was in the Jeep, parked outside the lodge.

How to get it?

Then she heard the sound of a car approaching. She ran to the window and saw the Jeep pull up outside the lodge. She saw Perry get out, carrying a plastic sack, and enter the lodge.

She stared for a long moment at the Jeep, knowing she

couldn't get to it and get her handbag. She heard voices, and moving silently, she opened the bedroom door and listened.

She heard Perry say, 'I want to talk to my wife.'

Brown said something, then a door shut and she heard no more.

Wait! she told herself. The time must come. The gun is there. Just wait.

Hollis switched on his radio.

'Sheriff?'

'Listening.'

'A bit of a mess. I suspect my cover is blown.' Briefly, Hollis went on to explain about the dog. 'This punk is no fool. He'll guess I'm up this tree,' Hollis concluded.

'Hell. I'd better tell Jenner, Hank.'

'No! As soon as it's dark, I'll move to another tree,' Hollis said. 'Don't worry about it. This punk won't show himself before it's dark, and maybe he won't even do that.'

'Look, Hank, it won't be dark. I've checked. There's a full moon tonight.'

'So fine. He has only to show himself and I'll nail him, but I just wanted you to know. I'll keep in touch.'

'You're sure you don't want me to come down there?'

Hollis forced a laugh.

'No, Sheriff, I can handle it. I've been in much worse spots in the Army,' and he switched off.

He eased his aching back against the tree-trunk and shifted his rifle. Already the sun was sinking. There was a blood-red glow on the river. In another half hour, the moon would come up.

He looked at the lodge. Lights had come on behind the drawn curtain. He wondered what was going on inside those walls. Leaning forward, he inspected a nearby tree. It would be easy to climb, but the sighting from up there wouldn't be as good as from the one he was in.

He'd wait, he thought. If Logan suspected he was up in the tree, there was a chance he would come out shooting.

Hollis fondled his rifle.

The moment the sound of the barking dog came to Perry and Brown, Brown, moving with the speed of a striking snake, was on his feet, gun in hand and at the window.

The speed of his movement stunned Perry. It seemed incredible that any man could move that quickly. He remained in his chair, watching, as Brown gently parted the curtains and stared out.

Perry listened to the savage barking of the dog. He was sure the dog had spotted the cop up in the tree. Now, what was going to happen?

There was a long pause. Then Perry heard a man's voice call to the dog. For some seconds, the dog continued to bark, then the man called again, and the dog ceased to bark.

Perry looked at Brown's thick, muscular back, at his blond hair and his evil crouch. His mind became active. He had to help this cop, hidden in the tree.

'Don't get excited, Jim,' he said, forcing himself to sound casual. 'This happens all the time.'

Brown pushed the curtains together and looked around, staring at Perry. His expression was so vicious, Perry felt a qualm.

'Watcha mean?' Brown snarled. 'That dog spotted a cop hidden in that tree. You think I'm a fucking idiot?'

'That dog spotted an opossum. They are always up those trees.'

'A what?'

'Opossum. An animal. Dogs hate them,' Perry lied, forcing a casual note into his voice. He searched for a cigarette, then lit it. 'You have cops on the brain. I well remember, last time I was here, I saw a number of these animals, tree-climbing.' Watching, he saw Brown was relaxing. 'They are like big rats. They feed on fish and eggs. You've heard of opossums, haven't you?'

'Yeah?' Brown moved away from the window. He now seemed totally relaxed as he shoved the gun back into its holster, but the evil grin and the uneasy darting of his eyes remained. 'So you don't think there is a cop: that tough-looking Deputy up there in the tree?'

'I told you, Jim,' Perry said quietly, 'I saw him less than two hours ago in Rockville. For God's sake! Relax!'

Still Brown stared at him.

'You could have driven him here, couldn't you? You could have left him in the goddamn forest to climb that tree, couldn't you? You could be lying, couldn't you?'

Perry tipped ash off his cigarette into an ashtray. He was surprised how steady his hand was.

'This is like a scene out of one of my movies,' he said. 'Of course I could be lying to you, Jim. I understand your suspicions. Frankly, it's great background for my movie.'

'Fuck your movie!' Brown snarled. 'Are you lying to me?'

Here, Perry felt he was on safe ground so he was able to say with confidence, 'No, Jim, I'm not lying to you. I did not bring the Deputy here. I didn't meet him.'

Brown continued to stare at him.

'An opossum, huh?'

'That's right. Now, Jim, can I go talk to my wife?'

The light in the room was darkening, now the sun had set. Neither of the men could see each other clearly. Perry switched on a table-lamp.

'Okay,' Brown said. 'No tricks, Perry. I like you. You're straight with me. I'll tell you something. Ever since I was in this goddamn world, no one but you has been straight with me. That's great, isn't it? No one. Even my pa wasn't straight with me. My mother wished I'd never been born. My Cobra pals secretly hated me, but you . . .' He suddenly smiled. It wasn't the evil grin Perry was now used to. It was a broad, almost innocent smile that made Perry feel ashamed of himself. 'So, okay, go talk to your wife. I'll get supper. Grilled prawns, okay?'

Perry heaved himself out of his chair.

'Fine.' He started for the door, then paused. 'You intend to leave tonight, Jim?'

'That's it. When it gets dark, I'll take off.' Brown said.

I guess I'll head for Jacksonville, then get lost. It's easy to get lost with ten grand. I've got lost on nothing, but this one will be dead easy.'

'I wish you luck,' Perry said, wondering if he meant this.

'I don't want anyone's luck . . . only my own,' Brown said. 'Go talk to your wife. If anyone wants luck, you do,' and he went into the kitchen and closed the door.

As Perry walked into the big bedroom, Sheila spun around and ran to him.

'Oh, darling!' She flung her arms around him in a hugging embrace.

Perry fondled her, feeling the tenseness of her back muscles.

'Are you all right?'

She pushed away from him, and they looked at each other. It startled him to see her hard, set expression and the stormy look in her eyes.

'All right? Yes, if you mean I had no trouble with that ape. What's happening?'

He closed the door.

'But there's something bothering you?'

'Oh, for Christ's sake! I've been waiting for you for hours! Don't you call that something?'

'I'm sorry. I've been getting information. I've things to tell you.' Lowering his voice, Perry went on, 'He's leaving soon after dark.'

'Leaving?'

'Yes. He's just told me. He's using the Jeep and driving to Jacksonville.'

Sheila stiffened. This overpowering urge to kill Brown dominated her thoughts.

You are, to me, like the mess a dog leaves on the sidewalk.

Those words continued to burn in her mind. If this brute got away, she could imagine him telling his friends what he had said to her. She could imagine their brutal, filthy laughter.

Seeing Perry was looking uneasily at her, she nodded. 'Well, that's something, isn't it?'

'It will mean we will be out of this nightmare.' He forced a smile. 'We can return to square A. Please, try to relax. This time tomorrow, we can begin our lives together again.'

'You talk the most utter drivel!' she snapped. 'Do you imagine our lives, after this, can go on as before?'

'I don't see why not. I love you, Sheila. We could make a new start.'

She stared at him.

'Use that corny dialogue for your next movie!'

'Sheila!'

She made an effort to control herself.

'I shouldn't have said that. I'm het up. We can talk about our lives when that stinking ape has gone.' She looked at him, her eyes calculating. 'You forgot my handbag, Perry. I need it. It's in the map pocket on the driver's side. Will you get it?'

'I'm damn sure Brown won't let me go out there, Sheila. Your handbag has to wait.'

'Well, try. I need my handbag.'

'Why?'

Her control slipped and, before she could stop herself, she blurted out with vicious fury, 'Because I'm going to kill that bastard! There's a gun in my handbag!'

Immediately she had said this, she regretted it. Why couldn't she have kept control of herself? Looking at Perry, seeing his expression, she knew he was more than shocked.

Then quietly, in that infuriating gentle voice he always used when she was in a difficult mood, he said, 'Now, Sheila. Come on! You know you haven't a gun.

That voice, attempting to be soothing, sparked off her rage again.

'I've got your gun! I took it from the safe! It's in my handbag. Go and get it!'

They were both talking in whispers.

'What are you doing with my gun?'

149

'You want to know?' Sheila faced him, her fists clenched, her eyes like glowing embers. 'I'll tell you. Your boss, that sonofabitch Hart, sicked a private eye on me! Do you like that? A filthy shamus who tried to blackmail me! Your boss, Perry! He did that to me! I had this creep in our home. He wanted ten thousand dollars. I fixed him. I got the gun from the safe and I shot at him. I scared the crap out of him! I wish now I had killed him as I intend to kill that ape!'

As Perry stood motionless, staring at her, into his mind came the words that Silas S. Hart had said to him:

I know her a lot better than you do. I've had reports on her background and reports of what she is doing while you try to write something worth while. My people bugged the motel where she has it off.

Perry had refused to listen, although he knew it was true. He still didn't want to accept the brutal fact that his wife was behaving like a tramp.

'All right,' he said, his voice husky. 'We'll go into all that later. This is not the time.'

'You sicken me!' Sheila exclaimed. 'Go and get my handbag!'

'You either don't understand or you won't believe the situation we're in,' Perry said quietly. 'This man is crazy in the head. I've already warned you the only way we can survive is to go along with him. If I asked his permission to get your handbag, he would want to know why. What do I tell him? You want your lipstick? He's not only crazy, but he's cunning. Maybe he would let me get the handbag. He would snatch it from me and find the gun. He would only need that to go over the edge. He would kill us as he killed six other people. We do nothing. Sheila. We wait. When it's dark, he will leave.'

Then they heard Brown call from the bottom of the stairs.

'Chuck's up! Come and get it!'

'We had better go,' Perry said. 'We must not antagonise him.'

She sneered.

'You go, spineless. I wouldn't eat anything that ape has touched. You go and keep your loony pal company.'

She turned and went to the window, looking out at the growing darkness.

Perry hesitated, then shrugged. He knew it was essential to keep Brown on even keel. Maybe there would be only a few hours before he left. He walked down the stairs into the living-room.

Brown, whistling tunelessly, was setting the table for three.

'Not my wife, Jim,' Perry said. 'Excuse her. This has been a shock to her. She's gone to bed.'

'Sure. I've always said the best place for a woman is in a bed.' Brown grinned. 'So okay, all the more for us, huh?'

Perry sat at the table. At all costs, he thought, he must keep this man on even keel. He had no appetite, but he must force himself to eat.

Brown returned with a steaming platter of rice in a curried sauce and big king-sized prawns laid on top.

'Looks good, huh?' he said, and helped himself generously, then pushed the platter towards Perry. 'I never told you, did I?' He began to eat savagely. 'One time, I was a short-order cook in a greasy spoon. I was a kid then. There was this black chef. He was gay, and he took a liking to me. When I first got there, I washed dishes, then he tried the old razzmatazz. So what did I have to lose? We had a few nights together. It paid off.' Brown munched while he stared in space. 'My old man was always saying crappy things, but one thing did stick in my mind. He was always saying "what you put in, you take out." ' Brown gave a barking laugh. 'He wasn't talking about gays. He meant something different.' Brown laughed again. 'Well, it paid off: this fag taught me how to cook. Pretty good, huh?'

Toying with the food, Perry said, 'Couldn't be better.'

'Yeah.' Brown had finished his portion of prawns. 'You ain't eating.'

'I'm fine.' Perry made an effort and swallowed some rice.

Brown stared at him.

'You worried about something?'

'I wish to God my wife hadn't come!' Perry said quietly. 'She's a complication, but I promise you, Jim, she won't be a nuisance.'

Brown helped himself from the platter.

'Right. I thought you might be worried about that opossum up in that tree.'

Perry felt a cold chill run through him. Had Brown seen through his lie? He forked a prawn and began to eat it.

'Opossum? Oh, that? Why should I worry about a tree animal? No, I'm worried about my wife.'

'Yeah That's natural.' Brown was silent, eating steadily. When finished, he eyed the prawns and rice. 'You want that, Perry?'

'No, thanks. I've had all I want.'

'Another of my old man's crappy sayings was never waste a thing.' Brown shoved the remaining food onto his plate. 'I bet you were never hungry. I know what real hunger is. There was a time when I hadn't a nickel. I starved. I used to walk the streets and pick over the trash-bins. That's how hungry I was. I used to walk along the streets where the restaurants were and peer through the windows, watching rich fat slobs stuffing their guts. I remember watching a slob who ate enough to last me a week. He had the lot: soup, fish, a big steak, two shots of apple pie. I remember him well. I can see him now. I watched him take out a wallet stuffed with money. That was my first mugging. I hit him. It was a pleasure. From then on, Perry, I never starved.'

'You've had a rough life, Jim,' Perry said quietly, pushing aside his plate.

Brown finished his meal.

'Not any more. With ten thousand dollars, I'm going to have a ball.' He looked up and grinned at Perry. 'You finished?'

'Yes, thanks. It was very good.'

'I'll clear the dishes. I like leaving things ship-shape. That's another of my old man's crappy sayings. Ship-shape, huh?' Brown gave his barking laugh. He gathered up the dishes and went into the kitchen.

Perry stood up, lit a cigarette and went to the window. He parted the curtains and looked out. It was dark. All he could see was his own reflection in the window glass. Replacing the curtains, he walked to a lounging-chair and sat down.

How much longer? he thought, listening to Brown's tuneless whistling and to the clatter of dishes as he washed up. So far, he seemed to be keeping this man on even keel, but the strain was beginning to tell on him. His hands were clammy, and his heart was beating unnaturally fast.

Then the sound of the telephone bell startled him.

Brown appeared in the doorway, his hand on his gun.

'Answer it, Perry,' he said. 'Careful. No tricks.'

Perry got to his feet and lifted the receiver.

'Yes?'

'That you, Boy?' He recognised the voice of Silas S. Hart.

'Hello there, Mr Hart.'

'How's it coming, Boy? You settled in nice? I guess you have had some tough weather your way.'

'Yes, but it's cleared now.'

'Good. Got an idea yet?'

'I'm working on something. Early days.'

'Sure. I'm not pressing you. You'll come up with something good. I'm relying on you. Done any fishing?'

'Not yet.'

There was a pause, then Hart went on. 'Had a call from Franklin. He wanted this contract fixed.'

'There's time. It's okay, Mr Hart, Don't worry about the contract. I'll sign it, but I don't want Franklin around for the moment.'

'Sure.' Again a pause. 'Your wife's joined you.' It wasn't a question, it was a flat statement.

'Yes.'

'That wise?'

Perry felt a surge of irritation.

'That's my affair, isn't it, Mr Hart?'

'I sure hope it is, Boy,' Hart said, his voice cold. 'Well,

okay. Let me know what you've come up with. So long,' and he hung up.

Perry replaced the receiver.

Brown, still in the doorway, was watching him.

'Your boss?'

'Yes.'

'You know something? I wouldn't work for anyone now. It's a sucker's game.'

'Most people have to work for someone, Jim.'

'Oh, sure. Suckers! Know something? If I worked for a jerk, and he told me what to do, I'd ram his teeth down his throat.'

'Then the jerk would be lucky not to employ you, wouldn't he?'

Brown grinned.

'You sure said something. Okay, in an hour or so, I'll be taking off. I reckon I've got a good chance. Once I get to Jacksonville, I'll get lost. No cop is going to catch me.' He patted the gun in the holster. 'With all that money, I'll leave them standing.'

'For your sake, I hope so.'

Brown regarded Perry.

'Yeah. Okay, go up and join your wife. I'm going to lock you in. When I'm ready, I'll let you know. I've things to do first. Come on!'

Perry walked from the living-room and up the stairs. He hoped, if he showed no resistance, didn't antagonise this man, he would go without harming either Sheila or him.

Brown followed him.

As Perry walked into the bedroom where Sheila sat on the bed, her chin in her hands, staring down at the carpet, Brown slammed the door, and Perry heard the key turn in the lock.

Hank Hollis switched on the radio.

'Sheriff?'

'Listening.'

'You were right. There's a full moon coming up fast. It's already lit up the river. In ten minutes or so, it will light the lodge. I've changed my mind. It would be too risky to change trees. I don't know if Logan suspects I'm up here, but it's safer to think he does. I don't think he'll risk coming out in the moonlight. The advantage is mine. If he does come out, I'll nail him. There's a big patch of flat ground before my tree. He'd have to cross it, so I'm staying where I am.'

'Hank! Hadn't I better come down? Extra fire-power. I'll be careful. I'll come by the footpath. I want to come.'

'With respect, Sheriff, don't. I've handled situations like this before. This is a one-man show. If I thought you were around and I heard you, I wouldn't know if it was Logan. You understand? I would hesitate to shoot and that could be fatal. So leave this to me.'

There was a pause, then Ross said, 'I understand. I'll stand by. Get in touch with me every ten minutes, and that's an order!'

'Okay, Sheriff. It'll work out.'

'Good luck, Hank.'

'If anyone needs luck, it will be Logan,' Hollis said and switched off.

Brown stood in the kitchen, an evil smile on his face.

An opossum?

Oh, yeah?

He was sure that tough-looking Deputy was up there in the tree, with a rifle, waiting for him. Well, okay, he had to get rid of him before he made his break.

He stood for some minutes, thinking. He pulled the gun from its holster, checked it, satisfied himself it was fully loaded and returned it to its holster. Then he turned off the kitchen light and went to the small window and peered into bushes and darkness. So far the moonlight was only flooding the front of the lodge. In another few minutes, the bushes at the back of the lodge would be lit.

Time to go.

He opened the window, got up on the sink, then slid out with the speed of a striking snake. Reaching the ground, he lay flat, listened, then, using his elbows to propel himself, he worked his way into cover. For several minutes he lay motionless, feeling the damp soil through his shirt. He waited until his eyes grew more accustomed to the dark, then he began to move forward again. Using his elbows and the toes of his boots, he moved forward as silently and almost as swiftly as a snake. He kept moving to his left, away from the tree where he was sure the cop was concealed. His planning was to make a circle and come up on the tree from behind.

When he was at right angles to the tree, now some fifty yards away, he paused. From where he lay, with the leaves of a shrub touching his head, he had a clear view of the tree. All he could see was dense foliage in spite of the now brilliant moonlight.

He nodded to himself. The cop had picked a good spot. He would be up in the top branches from where he would get a good sight of the lodge.

Brown waited. Sooner or later the cop would make a movement. Once he knew where he was, the rest would be easy. Brown settled down to wait.

Hollis eased his aching back. His rifle lay across his knees ready for instant action, his eyes were fixed on the lodge. Lights showed in the living-room and one upper room. He looked at the Jeep, now brilliantly lit by the moonlight. Logan would have to come out to get into the Jeep. Hollis was confident that he could nail him the moment he appeared. It was Vietnam all over again, but with a difference. Then, his back didn't ache. He wondered with a feeling of lost confidence, how long he could remain, straddled across the tree trunk. He shifted slightly to ease his back and the burning soreness between his buttocks. Come on, you punk! he thought. Show yourself! The silence and the lifelessness of the lodge depressed him, but he told himself, any moment there would be action. He fingered his rifle, then remembered the Sheriff's instructions to contact him every ten minutes. He switched on the radio.

'Sheriff?'

'What's happening?'

'Nothing so far.' Hollis held the receiver close to his

lips. 'I'm sure he'll break out sometime tonight. It's just a matter of waiting.'

'But, Hank, you've been up that tree for more than seven hours. How are you making out?'

Hollis forced himself to say, 'I'm okay. I could stay up here all night. I feel in my bones, Logan will break out tonight. Don't worry about me.'

'You're a fine man, Hank. I admire you,' Ross said.

Hollis smiled. Coming from an old cop like Ross this was high praise. He stiffened his aching back.

'Thanks, Sheriff. I won't let you down.'

'Call me in ten minutes. I'll be at the radio until you have nailed this punk.'

'Okay,' and Hollis switched off. Not once during their brief talk had he taken his eyes off the lodge. What was going on in there? Then a thought dropped into his mind. If Logan was going to break out, he would disconnect the telephone. Hollis couldn't accept the thought that this man would kill the Westons before he left. He would probably tie them up, disconnect the telephone and take off. Hollis hoped to God he was thinking right.

Unaware that Brown was creeping through the bushes, pushing himself forward by his elbows and toes and slowly circling the tree. Hollis switched on the radio.

'Sheriff, I've thought of something,' he said. 'If Logan is breaking out, he'll disconnect the telephone. Will you call Weston? If he answers, say it's a wrong number. I want to know if the telephone is disconnected.'

'Okay, Hank. Hang on.'

There was a five-minute pause, then Ross said, 'There's no ringing tone. I guess the telephone is disconnected.'

Hollis nodded.

'Then he's on the move. Okay, Sheriff, I'm ready for him. Can't be long now.'

'Keep in touch, Hank.'

'Don't worry,' and Hollis switched off. He was now very alert, but his eyes remained fixed to the lodge.

By now, his clothes caked with mud, Brown had reached the back of the tree. He lay still for some moments, then began to move forward until he was within twenty yards of the tree. He peered upward. The foliage of the tree at the back was less thick, but still he couldn't spot Hollis, so he waited.

The burning between Hollis's legs was becoming unbearable. He cursed himself for not bringing a blanket to make a saddle across the branch. How much longer could he stay in this position? He now knew the telephone had been disconnected. Any moment now, Logan would appear. His eyes still on the lodge, he carefully laid his rifle across two upper branches, then eased himself away from the branch he was sitting on, sucking his breath in relief.

That movement was fatal. Brown saw him. With an evil grin of triumph, he drew his gun.

Sheila looked up and stared at Perry, her eyes hostile. She stiffened a little as she heard the door lock snap shut.

'Now, what?' she demanded.

'He's getting ready to leave,' Perry said. 'With luck, this nightmare could be over in an hour.'

'Well, at least it will give you a movie plot, won't it?'

'Oh, Sheila! Can't you think about *us*?' Perry said, coming further into the room. 'Once this is over . . .'

'Oh, stop it! While you were eating that ape's food, I've been doing a lot of thinking. I have decided I have a very small place in your life. All you really think about is your stupid movie plots!' Sheila snapped. 'I'm a goddamn ornament to you! I decorate your home. You swell your stupid chest with pride that you have caught a young wife. Your only interest in me is when you get into bed! I know! There are many times when I talk to you and I know you're not listening! All you think about is money!'

Wearily, Perry sat down.

'Now, Sheila, this is not the time to start a domestic brawl. You must get it into your head that we are in a very dangerous situation. Brown is leaving. He could come up here and kill us both. Don't you understand? What has he to lose? I've done my best to keep friendly with him. He might be content to keep us locked in here. I hope to God he will, but until he leaves we both are hovering between life and a violent end.'

'Anything to shut me up!' Sheila exclaimed. 'I'm telling you, when this is over, I'm getting a divorce. I've had enough of you! I want my freedom! There are hundreds of men with more money than you who will go for me! I know! I've had enough of living with a script-writer! Understand?'

Perry looked at her and saw the cold implacable expression in her eyes.

This was the solution. He thought of those two years he had put up with this girl, doing everything he could to please her, but realising there were so many times when he was absorbed in his work and he had forgotten her. Writing for the movies was his life. He was dedicated to his talent. Yes! He immediately realised to be free from this girl would be more than a blessing. Yet, he felt defeated. He had tried desperately to make his marriage a success, but he should have known it was doomed to failure. Well, he knew now. It was over, and he felt a sense of relief.

He smiled at Sheila.

'If that's what you want, Sheila, all right. I'll arrange a divorce. I'll see you are taken care of.'

'Oh no, you won't!' Sheila said, her voice hard. 'I'll do all the taking care! If you imagine I've wasted two good years of my life, living with you, you're making a big mistake! I want the house. I want half your earnings! I'll take care of it!'

'Spoken like the child you are,' Perry said. 'All right. When we get out of this mess, we'll talk about it. Now please, relax. If you believe in God, now is the time to say a prayer. We could both be dead in a very short time.'

'What corny dialogue! Keep that for your movie script! When that ape leaves, I'm going to leave. I'm going back home, and I'm going to pack everything I own! You stay here in your stinking little lodge! I'm going back to Pa.

He'll put one of his smart attorneys on you, and between us we'll skin you! Make no mistake about that!'

'You haven't left yet,' Perry said. 'You may not leave.'

'Still trying to scare me?' She gave a hard, bitter laugh. 'I don't scare as easily as you.'

'I'm just warning . . .'

He broke off as both heard the sound of a gun.

Sheila's eyes opened wide.

'What was that?'

'Gun-fire. What did you think it was? A goddamn hiccup?' Moving swiftly, Perry snapped off the light, then went to the open window. His heart was hammering as he looked towards the big tree where he was almost sure the cop was hiding. The tree was lit by the moon. He saw the foliage move violently. Then to his horror, he saw a khaki-clad body tumble from branch to branch and land at the foot of the tree. A moment later, a rifle came spiralling down.

He drew back.

'He's killed the policeman,' he whispered.

Sheila ran to his side.

'Policeman? What are you talking about?'

Roughly, he shoved her back.

'This is trouble, Sheila. Prepare yourself.'

Still at the window, he saw Brown appear from the bushes. He could see him clearly in the bright moonlight. Brown was covered with thick mud. He paused for a long moment to stare down at Hollis's body, then he kicked Hollis's face savagely with his mud-encrusted boot, then he turned and began to run towards the lodge.

'Put on the light,' Perry said huskily. 'Sit down. Now listen. This is our only chance. Do exactly what he says. Understand?'

'You mean he's killed someone?' Sheila said as she switched on the light.

'There was a cop up in the tree across the way, waiting for him to come out,' Perry said. 'Brown found him and has killed him.'

The colour drained out of Sheila's face as she sank on the bed.

'Oh, God!' she muttered. 'Why did I come?'

'Quiet!' Perry snapped. 'Get hold of yourself! Listen!'

They heard the front door slam open, then slam shut. They heard Brown come thudding up the stairs. He thudded past their door and ran into the spare room.

They looked at each other.

'Don't make a sound,' Perry whispered. 'He may be leaving. He may not come in here.'

Listening, they heard the shower running.

'He's washing.'

Sheila shivered.

'If he comes in here, I'll scream the place down.'

'You'll do nothing of the kind! Antagonise him, and he'll kill us!'

'You've got to get me out of this!' Sheila whispered. 'You've got to protect me!'

'Listen!'

The shower had stopped running. They could hear Brown's tuneless whistle. They waited for more than five minutes, then they heard thudding feet along the passage that stopped at their door.

'He's coming in,' Perry said. 'Now, get hold of yourself!'

The lock snapped back and the door slammed open. Brown, wearing one of Perry's white shirts and a new pair of jeans, stood in the doorway. He looked at Sheila, crouching back, and then at Perry, forcing himself to relax as he sat in the armchair. Brown moved further into the room.

'I killed your opossum, Perry. A smart animal. It had a rifle and a radio. Real smart. What do you know?'

Perry tried to find words, but words wouldn't come.

'I'm off, Perry. I'm heading for Jacksonville. I'm taking a chance, but I guess I'll beat them.' The evil smile was in evidence. 'We'll say good-bye. I like you. Everyone makes mistakes. You thought there was an opossum up there, but I didn't, and I was right. Let's shake hands, Perry. Maybe you feel like wishing me luck.'

Perry got unsteadily to his feet.

'I do wish you luck, Jim. Will you be all right for food? Do you want anything from the freezer?' Perry was forcing himself to speak calmly.

'I don't need a thing. I've got money. I've got a gun, and I've got the Jeep.' Brown held out his hand. 'So it's goodbye.'

Perry forced himself to cross the room so he faced Brown who continued to smile evilly. He hated to touch this killer, but he had to do it. He clasped Brown's hard sweaty hand. His hand was gripped in steel-like fingers, crushing his fingerbones. He felt himself being jerked forward. As he was off balance, Brown hit him with his left fist on the side of his jaw. Perry went down as if he had been pole-axed. It was a terrible blow that sent him into black unconsciousness.

Sheila, her hands to her mouth, released a stifled scream. She didn't dare move. She sat staring down at her husband. Utter terror gripped her as Brown stepped around Perry's body and regarded her.

'Come on, baby,' he said. 'You and me are going places. You start tricks and I'll break your neck.' He reached for her and jerked her to her feet. 'You're doing the driving. As long as I have you with me, the cops won't shoot. Come on!'

Her legs scarcely supporting her, his hand gripping her arm, she was bundled down the stairs and out into the moonlight. She was forced into the driving-seat of the Jeep. Brown ran around and climbed into the passenger's seat.

'No tricks, baby. Just drive.'

'I don't think I can,' Sheila said breathlessly.

'Too bad. Drive or I'll slap you. I'll loosen your goddamn teeth!'

With a shaking hand, Sheila turned on the ignition. The Jeep started with a jerk.

'Make for the highway,' Brown said. 'Get moving!'

Mary Ross came into the Sheriff's office with a fresh pot of coffee and a thick slice of apple pie.

'Jeff, dear,' she said quietly, putting the coffee and the pie on his desk, 'you've been sitting here without your supper for the past seven hours. Why not take a rest? I'll take over, and if Hank calls, I'll call you. Now, come on, Jeff, you'll be fit for nothing if you go on like this.'

Ross turned and looked at her. She was shocked to see how he had aged and how haggard his face was.

'Hank's been up that tree for as long, Mary,' he said. 'I don't quit until this business is settled. Anyway, thanks for the coffee. I don't want the pie.'

'Take a bite,' Mary urged. 'It's your favourite. It'll do you good.'

'Don't fuss!' There was a bark in Ross's voice. 'This is my job, Mary!' He looked at the wall clock. 'I told Hank to call me every ten minutes. It's now a quarter of an hour since his last call.'

'It's you who are fussing, Jeff,' Mary said. She poured the coffee, added sugar and pushed the cup towards him. 'Give him a little time. Something might have happened.'

'Yes? But what? Something might have happened to Hank! That Logan is as dangerous as a cobra.'

'Drink some coffee,' Mary said soothingly. 'Would you like me to put a drop of Scotch in it.'

Ross sipped the hot coffee.

'No! I keep thinking of Hank up there, alone. You know, Mary, he's a fine man. The best deputy I've ever had.'

'I know. Be patient, Jeff. You see, it'll come out all right.'

Ross wasn't listening. His eyes were riveted on the wall clock, watching the big minute-hand crawl around.

'He's overdue by nearly twenty minutes,' he muttered. 'I'll give him another three minutes, then I'm calling him.'

'Would that be wise, Jeff? You might be interrupting something.'

'I'm calling him,' Ross said firmly. 'I can't stand it, sitting here when Hank could be in trouble.'

As the minute-hand of the wall clock indicated that three minutes had dragged by, Ross switched on the radio.

'Hank?'

Only the slight crackle of static greeted him.

'Hank?' Ross raised his voice. 'Do you hear me?'

No answering voice that he longed to hear came to him. 'Hank!'

Nothing.

'His radio could have packed up,' Mary said. 'It happens, doesn't it?' She was watching with dread the way her husband's bulky body was stiffening. She knew the signs. 'Now, Jeff, please . . .'

Ross stood up, pulled his gun from its holster, checked it and returned it.

'I'm going down there, Mary. Now, don't fuss! This could be the awful business all over again when Tom got killed. I'm going to see.'

'But not alone!' Mary exclaimed. 'Call Carl. Get men down there! Now, Jeff, stop this!'

'Don't you realise Hank could be wounded? He could be bleeding! It'll take Carl more than an hour to get anything organised. I'm going.' He touched her shoulder, then, slamming on his Stetson hat, he ran out of the office and out to the patrol car.

Mary stood motionless, then, as she heard the car start up, she moved swiftly to the telephone. She hadn't been a policeman's wife for over thirty years for nothing. In any emergency, Ross had once told her, always keep your head. Never panic. With a steady finger, she dialled Carl Jenner's number.

Jenner had checked through all the reports coming from the State police in their hunt for Chet Logan. The hunt was still going on; the results negative. Logan must be miles away by now, he thought as he got to his feet. He now looked forward to returning home where his wife was keeping his supper hot.

Then the telephone bell rang.

Impatiently, he picked up the receiver.

'Jenner.'

'This is Mary Ross. Carl, please listen and don't interrupt. We're in trouble here, and we need fast action. Here's what has been happening.' Concisely, she told Jenner that both Ross and Hollis had suspected Logan was hiding in Perry Weston's fishing-lodge, how Hollis had staked out the lodge in a tree, how he then confirmed that Logan was indeed there, that Mrs Weston had arrived, and it was agreed to bring in extra help would mean both Weston's and his wife's deaths were certain.

Jenner had sat down, the receiver pressed to his ear, now and then muttering, 'Jesus!'

'Hollis has been up this tree for seven hours. Weston collected ten thousand dollars from the bank and returned to the lodge. Jeff is sure Logan, with this money, is going to break out. Hollis was going to shoot him as soon as he appeared. He has been keeping in touch with Jeff every ten minutes,' Mary went on. 'Now, there's no answer on the radio.' Her voice began to shake, but with an effort, she controlled herself. 'Jeff has just gone to find out what's happening. Carl! You must do something quickly! Jeff is an old man. If Hollis is dead, Jeff can't handle a brute like Logan. Please . . .'

'Take it easy, Mary. I've got men standing by,' Jenner said. 'We'll be down there in half an hour. Leave it to me.' He slammed down the receiver and switched on his radio.

With his blue light flashing, but no siren, Sheriff Ross drove down the highway at a breakneck speed.

At this hour, the traffic to Jacksonville was light. Seeing the flashing blue light, oncoming cars pulled to the side to let the patrol car flash by.

As he drove, Ross was thinking. He would stop at the footpath and make his way down the path to the river on foot. He was tempted to use the muddy road, but if Hank's radio had failed and Hank was still up the tree, arriving in the patrol car at the fishing-lodge would be a complete give-away. If he went by the footpath, he would be faced with a two-mile walk. He slowed the patrol car. He was rushing things, yet he kept thinking of Hollis. Then seeing the lights of a garage ahead, he gave a nod. A bicycle!

He pulled into the garage, and an elderly man came out, wiping his hands on an oil-stained rag.

'Evening, Sheriff,' he said. 'Fill her up, huh?'
'No, Tom. Have you a bicycle I can borrow?'
The man gaped.
'A bicycle?'
'Police business, Tom. Have you got one?'
Startled by the bark in Ross's voice, the man nodded.
'Sure. You want it?'
Ross got out of the patrol car and lifted the hatch back.
'Put it in there, fast!'

Within two minutes, the bicycle in the car, Ross was again roaring down the highway.

Reaching the signpost 'River' he pulled up, dragged the bicycle from the car, then walked with it to the footpath.

He couldn't remember how long ago it was since he had ridden a bicycle. It was said once you have ridden a bicycle you could always ride a bicycle, like swimming.

Ross mounted the machine, wobbled, thudded against a tree and nearly fell off. He righted the machine, cursing under his breath, then started riding. By sheer will-power, he kept the bicycle going. Then as the footpath straightened out he increased speed. He pedalled furiously, feeling sweat running down his face, practically throwing the bicycle forward.

Three times, he nearly hit disaster, as the bicycle skidded in soft patches of mud, but he managed to keep going. He was aware the minutes were passing. The two-mile ride would remain in his memory until his death. With his breath rasping through his clenched teeth, his heart hammering from exertion, he saw ahead of him, the glitter of the river in the moonlight.

Slamming on the brakes, he skidded to a standstill, then, dropping the bicycle into the shrubs, drawing his gun, he moved slowly and cautiously down the path.

He paused when he could see the fishing-lodge, brilliantly lit by the moonlight. He waited several minutes until his breathing returned to normal, then, crouching, he moved forward for several yards, then again stopped.

From where he was, he had an uninterrupted view of the lodge. He could see lights were on in the living-room and in the major bedroom, then he realised the Jeep had gone.

So Logan had taken off!

Straightening, he moved forward warily, then he saw the body of Hank Hollis, lying at the foot of the big tree.

Ross felt a cold, sick feeling of shock run through him. He moved quickly and knelt. He didn't have to touch Hollis to know he had lost the best deputy he had ever had. 'Oh, Hank!' Ross muttered. 'I'll get him if it's the last thing I do!'

Then he heard a sound that made him jump upright.

The front door of the lodge slammed open and Perry Weston came staggering out. He reeled, fell on hands and knees, then struggled to his feet. Moving like a drunken man, he staggered towards the garage.

Ross slammed his gun back into its holster and ran to Perry.

'Mr Weston!'

Perry turned, reeled and caught hold of Ross's shoulder for support.

'Jesus, Sheriff! The bastard's gone, and he's taken my wife as hostage!'

In the moonlight. Ross could see the black bruise on the side of Perry's face.

'Take it easy, Mr Weston,' he said. 'I'll get back to my car and send an alert. How long has he been gone?'

'Fifteen minutes, a little more.' Perry moved away from Ross. 'Where's your car? Come on! He's taken my wife as hostage!'

'Top of the road. I've got a bicycle . . .'

'We'll go in my car. Come on!'

Still unsteady, Perry half ran, half staggered to the garage and flicked on the light, then he paused and cursed.

He saw, before Brown had left, he had deflated both the rear tyres and they were on their rims.

'You stay here,' Ross said. 'I'll get her up to the top of the road,' and he slid his bulk into the driving-seat.

Perry snatched open the passenger's door and got in beside Ross.

'Get going!' he shouted.

Ross started the engine and backed out of the garage, the car juddering on its flat tyres.

Then began a nightmare drive of two miles to the highway. The road had dried out, but there was still mud. Rattling and juddering the car slid with Ross using all his strength to keep the car straight.

'He told me he was heading for Jacksonville,' Perry said. He was now recovering from Brown's punch. His jaw ached and he tasted blood in his mouth. His only thought was of Sheila.

The car slid and smashed into a tree. The offside wing of the car ripped off, but Ross swung out of the skid and kept on.

In less than ten minutes they reached the highway where the patrol car was parked. Switching off the engine, Ross scrambled out and ran to the patrol car. He switched on the radio. Moving more steadily, but slowly, Perry joined him.

Ross was talking to Jenner.

'Take it easy, Jeff,' Jenner said. 'Mary alerted me. I've got roadblocks set up. I've got twenty men who will be with you in fifteen minutes.'

'He's got Mrs Weston as hostage!' Ross snapped. 'He's heading for Jacksonville.'

'Tricky, huh?' Jenner said. 'I'll handle it,' and he switched off.

As Sheila manoeuvred the Jeep up the mud road, with Brown at her side, her panic began to subside. The steel core in her began to assert itself. She knew she was in mortal danger. If she didn't do something, she was as good as dead, and Sheila had no intention of dying. She was sure that Brown would eventually kill her when he had no further use for her as a hostage. She thought of the gun in her handbag in the map pocket, but how to divert his attention to give her time to grab the handbag and get the gun?

'Hurry it up!' Brown snarled. He was leaning forward, studying the mud-covered road in the light of the headlamps.

Sheila slightly increased speed. They were approaching the bad patch of mud where Perry had bogged down. Should she try to bog the Jeep down? That wasn't the answer. Brown would fly in a rage and hit her.

'Watch this!' Brown barked. 'Get up to your right and take it slow.'

She did as she was told, and they crossed the drying quagmire without trouble.

'You know something?' Brown said, easing himself back in his seat. 'For a chick, you drive all right.'

Sheila said nothing. She slightly increased the speed of the Jeep. Within ten minutes, they reached the junction of the river road and the highway.

'Stop!' Brown snapped. 'Turn your lights off.'

She stopped and snapped off the lights. They sat side by side in complete darkness. She could hear his heavy breathing and smelt the sweat on him.

Here, perhaps, was her opportunity. She moved her right hand from the steering-wheel and to the map pocket. A thought flashed through her mind. Suppose this ape had checked the Jeep and had found the gun? Her heart was hammering as her fingers moved further, and felt the hard outline of the gun. Dare she risk pulling the bag from the map pocket, grope for the zip fastener, open the bag and get the gun in her hand?

Brown said, 'Now take it easy. We're going to cross the highway. There's a dirt road opposite. We take that. As soon as the traffic gives us a break, you drive fast across the highway. Got it?'

'That's not the way to Jacksonville,' Sheila said, snatching her hand from the map pocket.

Brown gave a soft barking laugh.

'You know something, baby? I like your husband. He's a great guy. I told him Jacksonville because I didn't want to kill him. I hated hitting him, but I had to do it. Before long, the cops will arrive, and he'll tell them Jacksonville.' He laughed again. 'That way, the stupid bastards will set up roadblocks, but I'll be away in the forest!'

Sheila felt a cold chill run through her. By telling her

169

this, this ape was also telling her that before long he would kill her. She had to take a desperate risk if she was to save her life. While she was trying to think what to do, Brown was listening to the light traffic roaring along the highway.

'Get ready!' he snapped. 'Start the engine!'

She switched on.

Once across the highway and into the dense forest, he would make her stop, smash her head in, throw her body out and drive away.

'Right. Now move forward, dead slow,' Brown ordered.

She engaged gear and drove the Jeep slowly up to the entrance to the highway.

The sound of an approaching truck made him snap, 'Stop!'

She could now see the highway. The truck's lights made fast approaching pools on the road's surface. It went thundering by. Brown was leaning out of the window. No car lights showed either to their right or left.

'Now!' he said. 'Fast! Get across! Headlights!'

As she switched on the headlights, she saw, across the highway, a narrow opening to a road back into the forest. She aimed the Jeep at the opening and trod down on the gas pedal.

With the engine roaring, the Jeep surged across the highway and hit the forest road. She braked as soon as the Jeep began to bounce on the uneven, dirt road.

'Very sharp,' Brown said. 'Now take it easy. Keep going.'

Sheila didn't hear him. Her mind was busy. She was remembering what Perry had told her Brown had said to him: *We'll share a double funeral*. She remembered what Brown had said to her: *To me, you're like a mess a dog makes on the sidewalk*.

Okay, you stinking ape, she thought, if I'm going to die, you'll die with me!

She took a quick look at Brown who was sitting back apparently completely relaxed. He began his tuneless whistle.

She looked ahead, her eyes searching for a tree. The dirt road was bordered by dense flowering shrubs. Their scent

170

came into the Jeep's cabin. Then, with her heart beats quickening, she saw, in the headlights, a massive Cypress tree on the edge of the road, some hundred yards ahead.

Here it is, she thought. This is the end to both of us!

They were now travelling at thirty miles an hour. Bracing herself, she swiftly changed into the four-wheel drive and trod the gas-pedal to the floor.

The Jeep surged forward.

Sheila leaned back. Her hands gripped the steering-wheel. Her arms at full stretch.

'Hey!' Brown had only time to shout before she swung the Jeep towards the tree.

The Jeep, now moving at sixty miles an hour, smashed into the tree. There was a crunching sound of buckling steel.

Somehow, Sheila resisted the force of the smash. The violent jolt, for a brief moment, caused her to black out.

Taken unawares, Brown had been thrown forward. His head smashed against the windscreen. He was thrown back in his seat, unconscious.

Sheila came out of the blackout in a few seconds. For a long moment, she remained motionless, then she looked at Brown.

The light from the dashboard was still functioning. The big moon was also lighting the scene.

Oh, no, you ape! she thought. Not a double funeral!

She snatched her handbag from the map pocket and tore at the zipper. The zipper moved halfway, then jammed. With her eyes still on Brown, she tore at the bag's opening.

With frantic strength, she got the bag open, snatched out the gun as Brown shook his head and turned towards her. She pointed the gun at him and pulled the trigger. The gun banged. She saw him rear back in his seat. She fired again, then again. Each time Brown half reared up and fell back.

She saw small red blotches on his white shirt which blossomed into big patches of blood.

Triumphant, she leaned forward, staring at him. She watched him, blood now saturating his shirt. She saw him struggling to sit up. She saw his eyes open.

'Like it, Jimmy Brown?' she said breathlessly. 'Like it the way you killed decent, innocent people? Die! Suffer!'

Brown's eyes focussed. He stared at her. Blood began to dribble out of the side of his mouth. He tried to say something, but blood now began to pour out of his mouth, and he only made choking sounds.

'Go on, die, you stinking ape!' she screamed at him.

Gathering his enormous strength, his evil grin a grimace, Brown's left fist swung up. He hit Sheila a crushing blow on the side of her jaw. Her head snapped back, breaking her neck, and she slumped back on the seat of the Jeep.

They found them after a five-hour search.

When it was realised that Logan wasn't heading for Jacksonville, Jenner had diverted his men to search the forest.

Perry and Ross sat in the patrol car, listening to the police radio. Finally a voice came through.

'We've located the Jeep,' Jenner said, and gave directions.

Ross set the car in motion and, after a few minutes, drove up the dirt road. Perry sat still, his heart thumping. Ross pulled up where Carl Jenner was standing.

'It's over,' Jenner said.

Perry scrambled out of the car.

'My wife?'

'I'm sorry, Mr Weston. Better not go up there,' Jenner said quietly.

Perry brushed by him and ran the few yards to the wrecked Jeep.

Several State police were standing around. They just stood, watching.

Perry reached the Jeep and peered in.

He saw Brown, his eyes fixed in a defiant glare. Blood made him a horrible and grotesque figure. Perry's eyes moved to Sheila.

She lay back, his gun still in her hand. In death, her expression was almost serene.

THE END

172

>>> If you've enjoyed this book and would like to discover more great vintage crime and thriller titles, as well as the most exciting crime and thriller authors writing today, visit: >>>

The Murder Room
Where Criminal Minds Meet

themurderroom.com

9 781471 904127